# The Wilderness

ISBN-10: 0985667982
ISBN-13: 9780985667986

# The Wilderness

## Surviving the Unimaginable

Travis Wright

The will to survive, to fight and not give up is a basic human instinct. We only give up to save others or when we think that all hope is lost. We can do anything as long as we want it bad enough. Something to believe in can drive us beyond failure. "Pain is only weakness leaving the body," sounds good until it happens.

Travis Wright ( 2012 )

# Chapter One: Confusion

"Mayday, mayday! This is Cessna Two Four Seven Whiskey Romeo. We're going down. I repeat, mayday, mayday! This is Cessna Two Four Seven Whiskey Romeo. We are going down."

The plane, a rugged single-engine four-seater, widely used in Alaska, was bouncing all over the place and it wasn't because it was windy. Mike had never seen or heard of his Uncle Ted being as scared as he was right at that moment. His face was pale and beads of sweat were rolling down his right cheek. His hands were tightly gripping the yoke, with his knuckles bright red and almost poking through his skin. Ted was seventy-one years old, with a bald head and white moustache. He had flown and guided in Alaska's back country for over forty years, and his wrinkles showed his age.

Ted had been in a crash before and, from what he had told Mike, had stayed calm even when he hit the log on the beach as he landed and the plane flipped over in the water. As the plane hung upside down and filled with water, causing it to sink. He stayed calm and swam to shore after unbuckling, even though the icy springtime water stole his breath with every stroke. Too much exposure in the cold temperature could cause hypothermia to set in rather quickly and his quick thinking and experience saved his life that day.

Adding to Mike's fear, even more so than looking out the windows of the plane and seeing nothing, was that his uncle wasn't saying anything after the mayday he called in.

"Ted! What the hell's going on?" Mike shouted into the intercom of his headset, as he was being tossed around the plane. He tightened his seatbelt before being jostled further.

Mike had fallen asleep while the 206 was in the air on the way to the campsite. They had started going through Lake Clark Pass, a narrow corridor snaking between the rugged mountains on the west side of Cook Inlet, and then he was out. It had already been a long trip before he had even boarded the plane. When he woke up, a dense blanket of featureless white had enveloped them and he couldn't see the ground or the mountains.

Everything seemed as if it was in slow motion for a few seconds with a sudden snap back to reality.

"We were on our way through the pass when this fog set in," Ted said. "I don't know where we are now and we are losing altitude. I'm trying to figure out why."

Ted urgently continued to call mayday on the radio with no response, while adding and taking away throttle, trying to find the right speed at which to fly.

Mike could hear that they were about to stall by the sound of the engine. Ted had slowed the plane to a crawl so if they did crash, it might not be so bad. More than likely, at least there were no guarantees. This was what the small plane sounded like just before landing, and by this Mike knew they were in trouble, because they should be thousands of feet in the air.

Mike had intended for Ted to drop him off for spring brown bear hunting and pick him up a week later. Knowing the area pretty well, after being there previously and with his GPS, he figured he had a good chance of not getting lost. You can see for miles on the Alaskan tundra. If there are land-marks, like mountains, to aid you, Mike figured, then you really can't get lost. With all the gear he was bringing, including the satellite phone Ted had lent him, he felt confident he could handle any situation. He had learned a lot from the last trip.

Mike put his hand on Ted's shoulder. "Just take a breath and relax," he said.

The plane leveled out and started flying straight though still sandwiched in very thick fog all around the plane, cutting visibility to zero.

In an instant, the plane hit something and was skidding. Ted was yelling something on the radio that Mike couldn't really make out. The plane overturned violently after hitting something solid. Mike couldn't see much as he hit the side window and his gear was tossed around the cockpit. He glimpsed Ted fighting the controls and trying to shut the engine down. Mike covered his head and hoped nothing would hit him. He felt a sharp pain on the side of his head as he slammed into the window a second time. He saw a momentary white flash, felt searing pain, his hearing vanished and then everything slowly went black.

*"Code green, Mike code green,"* said a woman's voice.

Mike was looking around, trying to remember what code green meant. He was in a structure, but everything was hazy. It felt like he was in a meat locker, more specifically the freezer in the meat department at the grocery store. It was one of two places where he could put his mind at ease and shut out the entire world. The other, of course, was in his car during his forty-five minute commute to work every day.

The cold in the storage freezer never bothered him. In fact, he welcomed it. The industrial air conditioners throughout the store never seemed to work hard enough to battle the sticky California heat. Mike had never been a day dreamer, and although he spent roughly an hour each day idly standing in the freezer, to the amazement of the meat department manager and other employees, his mind never wondered too far from the cold. All 6'2" and 227 pounds of him just stood there, motionless, next to the solid flanks of frozen meat. He ran his hand over his thinning, short, black hair and wondered if his buzz cut was in need of a trim.

He started walking out of the freezer toward the voice repeatedly calling 'code green'. He had to find out what she was talking about. He rounded yet another corner of the never-ending aisles as he searched, and saw a young kid with baggy jeans and his cap on sideways standing in the middle of the aisle, with a mop. He was cleaning up green vomit deposited by the chubby little boy with the white face and red hair standing nearby.

*This must be the code green,* he thought. Mike was getting even colder, somehow, as he watched all of this unfold in front of him, but didn't feel alarmed by any of it.

"Give me the mop and go in the back to help Harold with the vegetables," Mike told the teenage kid, whose name escaped him.

Without a word, the kid walked down the aisle and disappeared. The green, half-eaten food wasn't coming up off the floor very well as Mike tried to clean it up, and what was that constant buzzing he kept hearing? *What had this kid consumed?* He stopped what he was doing and reached into his front right pocket to check his cell phone. Eleven missed calls from Rachael? This was puzzling, but he knew he didn't have time to call his wife back right then.

After finally getting the disgusting green substance off the floor, out went the "slippery when wet" signs, and the mop and bucket were stored in the back room once again.

Mike went off to check on the rest of the employees and make sure their jobs were being done to his satisfaction. There was still the question of the haze in the building, but this wasn't the main issue. Overseeing the work had to take precedence, a lesson he learned all too well after the recent surprise visit from corporate.

When he was finally able to take a break and call Rachael back, she didn't answer. He left a message and wondered if he should try again, but the little brunette with short hair and freckles from check-stand three wouldn't stop talking to him in her squeaky voice.

More employees came into the break room until it was completely full. They were all talking loudly and Mike was concerned that no one was downstairs at their stations where they needed to be. He left, pushing his way through all of them, and as he made it to the bottom of the stairs he could see the store was empty. Frantic, Mike walked briskly around the store and broke into a run. Still finding no one, he went outside to find an empty parking lot. There was in fact nobody to be seen anywhere.

As he walked through the front door of the supermarket, it was still very hard to see through the mist all around him. Mike heard crunching under his feet and looked down seeing snow. Before he could contemplate the sudden strangeness of the groundcover, he slipped on some ice and, fell, hitting the side of his head against the corner of an end cap-shelf.

# Chapter Two: Shock and Realization

Mike woke up and could barely feel his fingers. His nose and ears were stinging, while his lips felt wet. He was hanging upside down, wet snow caked to him. His head was pounding and his left arm ached. He didn't know how long he had been out for, but knew he was in trouble. He called out for Ted, but got no response. Mike could tell he was still in the plane, but everything was blurry, with very little light allowing him to see his surroundings. He felt like he was hungover and his head was cold, coated in something, blood, more than likely. As he reached up and felt his left eye, he determined that it was frozen shut from his own blood. He had to pick it away like an old scab to open it.

*What the hell was that dream about and what did it mean?* Mike wondered.

There were more important things to worry about. He knew this. Mike tried as hard as he could to focus. He finally unbuckled after pushing hard on the release button and fell to what was now the bottom of the plane. He shook his head trying to focus.

He remembered the plane slamming into something and rolling. They must have crash-landed, but with the fog so thick he had no idea where they were. Mike gathered himself up and brushed off the remaining snow. He pushed the button on his Chase-Durer watch that should have made it light up, but didn't.

"That's strange," he mumbled.

The watch was recommended to him by an acquaintance that had been an active-duty Navy SEAL. He said it was the best one to have in any situation.

The expensive watch being damaged was the least of his worries so he carefully picked his way toward the back of the plane, until he realized it was missing. Feeling around in the dark, digging through what was left, he found a parka among the scattered pieces of gear. He found two right-handed gloves and put them on anyway. Staying warm was his first priority, then he would find as much gear as possible before leaving the plane to look for his uncle.

Ted had mentioned before they left that the landing area was surrounded by quite a bit of melting snow, so Mike had put his Muck boots and Browning windproof and waterproof pants on before getting in the plane that afternoon, even though it had been warm and sunny on the airstrip. Otherwise he would have just had his camp shoes and jeans on. Mike knew Ted had flown out to the camp a day or two ahead of time, like he always did, to ferry supplies, repair anything on the camp that had fallen in from too much snow or got torn up by animals, and to take a general look around the area.

Mike located a headset and put it to his ear. Hearing nothing, he guessed from the silence that the electronics must have died when they crashed. This could mean that the emergency beacon may not be active, but he didn't know enough about planes to be sure. His cell phone was still in his pants pocket, but he doubted there would be any service on this side of the mountains. He took a glove off, pulled it out and turned it on, but was disappointed in correctly predicting no service as the display indicated.

Mike wondered how far they had gone, and how close they were to the camp. Ted would know, but where was he? Mike turned his cell-phone back off to conserve the battery. He continued to feel around and collect gear, while making a mental list of what he had.

"Not much yet," he said.

Mike had been on this spring brown bear hunt one other time and wasn't really looking forward to freezing his ass off again, but had been pleased to get away from reality for awhile. His current predicament was an unfortunate turn of events, to say the least, but he felt confident that when the fog lifted he could get his bearings.

He tried to remember the sequence of events leading up to the crash, but it was all still very hazy. Mike thought about what had happened from the time he woke on the plane until they crashed. He remembered a thick white blanket all around them that made it impossible to see. If he could just figure out where he was, he would feel more confident about the situation.

Mike knew one problem this time of year in the Alaska Interior was the minimal daylight. He and Ted had taken off from the airstrip in town mid-afternoon, knowing they would still have some light to work with even after the two hour flight to Ted's track of land he leased from the state that he used to guide from.

Night was falling. His watch told him it was just after 4:00 p.m. and without a flashlight and the thick fog, Mike couldn't see much around him. He crawled as far into the plane as he could and moved coolers and gear in front of him. Daylight was a long way off, but he pushed himself to hang on, hoping that the weather would lift and a search plane would find the crash-site. His mind continued to reel from the events of the day and he paused in an effort to develop a game plan.

Mike figured that the rest of the vital items he needed had ejected out of the plane when they crashed, and felt helplessness mounting in his search to find things for his continued survival such as a much-needed flashlight and items to keep him warm. Mike knew his cell-phone light would work, but didn't want to use up the battery.

He was still wearing his chest holster, even though Ted had told him to take it off in the plane, but his.44 magnum revolver had fallen out. Things were not looking very good at this point. He anticipated that with more light the next day it would be much easier to find the necessities they had brought like food, weapons, and the satellite phone.

Mike found a duffel bag wedged beneath one of the seats and was able to pull it out. He took his gloves off and opened it up, feeling inside. There was a flashlight in it, but it wouldn't turn on.

"Matches, I have matches!" he exclaimed.

There wasn't much else useful in there that he could feel. He had to hope he would find more gear in the morning.

Mike would finally be able to see his surroundings with the matches, but didn't want to use too many of them because the box felt almost empty. There was no fuel smell so he felt confident he wouldn't blow up the plane and himself. He lit the first match and it immediately went out.

"Come on baby," he said.

The second match stayed lit, and he slowly moved it around the plane searching for anything that would help his situation. Just before the light was gone, he saw Ted and jumped back thudding his already pounding head on the fuselage. He quickly lit another match and turned to look behind him again.

To his horror, Mike saw Ted hanging behind him through the windshield of the small plane. He had somehow come out of his seatbelt and had turned completely around. His head was sticking through the windshield from the outside of the plane with a piece of his scalp pealed back. The match went out and Mike lit another to look at the scene again. Ted's mouth was wide open, his tongue dry and blue. His eyes were equally wide, unfocused and white as a cataract. There was blood from his wounds, frozen on his face and all around the immediate area. Mike knew he was dead, but checked for a pulse anyway. Not a beat, and he was cold.

"No! No! No! This can't be happening," Mike shouted at his lifeless uncle as the match burned down.

Mike must have been unconscious for a while after the crash. Could Ted have been suffering while he was out? The possibility didn't sit well with him. Mike closed Ted's eyes as the match went out.

Not only was his uncle dead, but Ted knew the whole area. He wasn't just his family, but a guide that Mike desperately needed. Mike felt comfort in the fact that he had found the man, but remorse also because he had died and Mike was more or less OK.

Mike was trying not to let it get to him, but when he started crying, it became real.

"This isn't supposed to be happening," he sobbed.

It was completely dark now and Mike decided to not waste any more matches. He needed a flashlight to look for more things, but would have to wait until daylight to look again. He knew he shouldn't have used so many matches and with his luck would end up regretting it later. Pulling the hood of the parka over his head, he tried to stay as warm as possible.

It was a cold and extremely long night. Besides the current circumstances, all he could think about was the fight that he and Rachael had had before he left. Just thinking about her and what or who she was doing at that moment was killing him. All he had were suspicions, but all those nights of her coming home late, taking a shower and going to bed without even a word said between them. He blamed himself if she was cheating. The life they were supposed to have all went away when he hurt his back his senior year and lost his college football scholarship. He tried to put this out of his mind too and get some sleep, but it repeated in his head. He loved her still, but hated what their relationship had become. He thought about following her and catching them together, but knew he couldn't handle that. He wanted to confront her, but what if he was just imagining it and he ruined his marriage by bringing it up because he didn't trust her?

The last thing a woman wants is a jealous husband, or so he read in that one magazine. The name escaped him, but it had a lot of good advice in it.

Mike woke so many times through the night that he lost count. The air was calm, keeping the blanket of fog locked in low to the ground for now, but at least he could retain his body heat a little easier. The last time he had gone on this hunt, the wind was so strong for days that it blew everything over.

The tents had remained staked to the ground but they were flattened by the wind even when they slept in them at night. With gusts over fifty miles per hour, they even had to tie the plane down to the ground. He hadn't gotten a bear because of the weather. Even so, the time away had been a nice change.

Mike wasn't a big hunter, but when Ted offered to take him for a minimal fee, he couldn't pass it up. Ted was retired from guiding, but maintained the land lease with the state in order to camp and hunt with friends and family. Mike had heard the stories of the caribou herd that used to roam the area. They numbered in the thousands and for more than ten years, the hunters that were flown out always got their trophies with Ted and his son, John, guiding them.

The sun didn't rise the next morning, it just got less dark out. The visibility was still very bad and Mike could only see a few feet in front of him after uncovering and looking out the nearest window. He hoped it would clear off, but feared it would stay for most of the day.

His left eye was still partially shut from the blow to the window, further obscuring his vision. He felt an urge to get out, move around and find as much gear as possible. He needed to get his blood circulating. He could barely feel his hands, and his feet weren't very warm either, even in the insulated boots.

*It would be so nice to be back home getting the boys ready for school and sipping hot coffee right now,* he thought.

The twins didn't listen to him like they used to, but he figured it was just them growing up and almost being teenagers. As he moved the coolers out of the way, he felt something on the bottom of the plane.

"My revolver," he yelled in excitement as he pulled it up to look at it.

The gun looked like it was still functional, but he couldn't be sure, as he wasn't very well versed in guns. He wouldn't know for certain until he fired it.

Mike moved out of the plane and still couldn't see anything but snow, ice and a few boulders and jagged rocks poking through it. They must have hit the top of the peak and slammed into some of the rocks. He consolidated all the gear he could find and went through it. He found a small flashlight that worked and wondered how long the batteries would last. The food supplies had spilled out on the ground and he scavenged what he could through the snow-covered mess. It wasn't much, but it was better than having nothing at all.

He took a break and ate some jerky and a granola bar. He hadn't eaten since lunch the day before and even though this wasn't much, he found himself ravenous. Mike savored every bite and chewed slowly to make it last longer. He wanted to keep up his strength, but was concerned about eating too much, as he didn't know how long this little bit of food would have to last before help came.

There was so much going on that he didn't even realize he hadn't had a cigarette for more than a day. He hadn't even wanted one until he remembered he smoked. He had found Ted's heavy jacket in the plane and not his own that had a partial pack of Camels and a lighter in it. Mike searched frantically for the jacket after feeling the overwhelming desire for nicotine, but didn't have any luck.

He knew the withdrawals would only last a few days, since he had quit before, though, inevitably started again with all the stress that his life brought him. He would look again in the plane and hoped he would find it or even a few cigarettes.

For now, Mike needed to move Ted's body away from the crash site just in case any animals came by. He didn't want them to eat Ted, but his body could bring them into the area and ultimately to him, Mike figured.

The snow was deep and hard to move in, but after much effort, he was able to move Ted's stiff body away from the plane about fifty feet. Mike had never seen a dead body before and it felt like he was moving a log with flopping branches. He covered it with a tarp and marked the spot with debris in case it was covered by blowing snow. It wasn't the easiest thing he had ever done, but he couldn't handle having Ted in there next to him for another night if he had to sleep in the plane again.

"When will this damn fog lift?" he said.

He continued to search the area but the supplies must have scattered over a large section of the mountain or were buried in the snow. The thought of walking down the mountain in search of more items and getting lost didn't sit well. Without being able to see very far in front of his face, Mike decided to stay close to what was left of the plane.

He secured the Cessna much better than it had been the first night, but there was still open areas letting the cold in and there was nothing he could do about it. Only half the plane was left. The tail section had broken off and Mike couldn't see it anywhere. He did the best he could with what he had in order to wait for rescue. Mike waited inside the plane as the daylight slowly left. There were no planes to be heard all day.

*The bad weather must be keeping them grounded,* he thought.

Mike tried to get some sleep and hoped that the nightmare he was living would soon be over. He slept fitfully throughout the night.

Mike woke up while was still dark. He had a bad feeling, and then heard again what had woken him in the first place. The growling wasn't too close, but he didn't like it anyway. Suddenly, he heard what sounded like a few dogs fighting. He didn't dare turn on the flashlight and instead gripped the.44 magnum revolver tightly as the growling, barking and whimpering, continued. It seemed like an eternity listening to what he knew were wolves. He couldn't understand why they weren't trying to get into the plane, but was glad they didn't.

Mike knew he was at a crossroads. There were many questions that needed to be answered. How big was the pack? Were they just passing through? He wanted to wait for rescue, but could he hold out that long? He didn't even know where he was.

Mike tried to stay awake and alert, but the dark would lull him to asleep and then the cold would wake him again with sharp pains in different parts of his body. He needed to move around to get circulation to his legs, but he dared not make any noise and alert any wolves that might still be in the area. He drifted in and out until it seemed lighter again.

He knew he needed to get off the mountain peak and to a lower and warmer elevation for shear survival and hopeful rescue. If he stayed in the plane, the cold or the wolves would be the end of him sooner than later.

The next morning, he could see a little better, but the white blanket was still all around. He noticed the tarp was ripped up and there was blood in the snow where he had put Ted. He didn't go near the area to investigate because he knew what he would find.

Mike laid out everything he scavenged from the plane and surrounding area. His Ruger Redhawk four-inch, stainless,.44- magnum revolver with nine shells, a flashlight, a skinning knife, a canteen partially full of water, half a box of matches, Ted's parka, the small duffel, two right-handed gloves and a few days worth of food, at best, were all he could find. He had no idea where the rest of the gear had gone when they crashed and knew he couldn't continue to look for it. With the wolves in the area, the cold temperatures and the limited visibility, he thought it would be more dangerous to stay.

*A rifle would be nice to have if the wolves come back,* he thought, but he hadn't found one during his search.

One last walk through of the plane while it was light out was something he had to do. With each passing day, about ten minutes more light would be added to aid him this time of year, but it wasn't enough yet. Mike got down on his knees when he got back to the plane and slowly moved what was left out of the way during his search. He still couldn't find his jacket and fell to the floor in agony.

"*A cigarette would taste real good right now*," he thought from the now bottom of the plane, looking up at the seats.

He saw something wedged between the back seats and reached up for it. A pack of Camels that had come out of his bag were virtually intact. With a big smile on his face Mike ripped open the pack and struck a match, lighting one up and inhaling like it was a fresh breath of air. He savored the taste and held in the smoke longer than normal before he slowly let it out, blowing a few smoke rings. He had brought a whole carton so he didn't run out. Now this one pack would have to last him.

Partially satisfied, he put everything he had in the small duffle bag he found in the plane, secured the revolver in his chest holster and looked around for the best place to get off the mountain.

As he walked by the plane he stopped and pulled off the spear-sized aluminum rod connecting the wing to the fuselage for support. It was already barely attached and came off easily. It would make a nice walking stick and weapon, if it came to that.

The visibility up on the mountain was still bad, but as Mike pushed his way through the deep snow, he was starting to be able to see farther in all directions. The cigarette was almost gone and he stopped to finish it on a large boulder on top of the snow.

Mike had wanted to hunt a big brown bear and hopefully get a full mount made. He talked to a taxidermist friend of Ted's about making the mount for him. He wasn't a big hunter, but after Ted had invited him over to his house while on vacation in Alaska and shown him all of his trophies, Mike made up his mind to go after the majestic animal. Rachel didn't want a bear in the house. She said it would scare her just knowing it was there. Mike realized he wanted it partially because she didn't. It would also be a great conversation piece when company was over.

The walk was slow in the snow and continued to be tough as it transitioned to rocks and then back to the white stuff. Mike still couldn't see very well out of his hurt eye, which slowed his decent.

He came across an area of fresh dirt and knew immediately what this sign meant from his previous trip to the area. He pulled his revolver out of its holster and moved to the left side of the bear den. There were large and small tracks all around the area in the dirt and snow. He could tell from the large and smaller prints that this was from a brown bear sow and a cub or two. They probably moved down the mountain to hunt and could be miles away by now, but he would be very cautious anyway. He'd been through enough already and didn't want to get in the way of the sow and her cubs. A raven was circling above and squawking. Mike didn't pay much attention to it and kept descending the rough terrain.

Once he got farther down into the valley he was navigating, he heard the rush of water and moved in its direction. The water was heading down with gravity and would meet up with a larger body of water a river, lake and eventually, the ocean, he reasoned.

The compass on his watch said he was heading southwest. There were hundreds of miles of uninhabited coastline in Alaska. Mike knew this, but it was his best chance at finding a small, remote village or another hunting camp and getting home. Some of the lakes would have cabins and possibly spring hunting camps around them, or even on the tundra like Ted's.

As he walked he tried to keep alert. With the snow melting, the bears and wolves would be out, and hungry. His arm and head were feeling better, but both still ached. The swelling on his eye was slowly going away. At least he could see out of it now. He was glad he sustained no injuries that would make walking impossible.

As he got closer to the stream Mike saw something moving on the terrain below. He positioned himself on a large rock so that he could see it better.

His heart was starting to beat faster as he saw what had caught his eye.

"Aah, food," he said softly.

# Chapter Three: The Plane

It was an arctic hare that still had its entirely white winter coat, and it was slowly making its way down the mountain, too. The small animal wasn't moving very fast and kept stopping to look around, twitching its nose and moving its ears. Mike took his skinning knife off his belt, and took out the draw-string on the parka's hood. He attached the knife to the end of the aluminum rod from the plane to make a spear, keeping an eye on the hare while he worked. Once he was satisfied the knife was secure, he made his way toward the small animal. Inching closer and trying to anticipate where it was headed, Mike was getting close.

Mike was on top of a small group of rocks right above the stream when he moved into position to thrust the spear into the hare. With the sound of the water to mask his approach, he nervously moved closer. His whole body tensed, his heart pounding in his chest like a jack hammer, Mike did his best to steady himself. In a burst of movement, he thrust downward. As fast as the spear entered the hare's body, its life ended. It never knew what hit it.

"I did it!" Mike yelled. "I can't believe it worked."

A huge smile on his face, Mike beamed with the pride of his accomplishment. As long as opportunities like this presented themselves from time to time, he would make it through this ordeal until helped arrived.

He cleaned the hare in the snow and filled his canteen in the cold water of the stream. It would be nice to boil the water before drinking it, but this would have to do. He hoped it was clean enough that he wouldn't get sick. Fatigue would be one thing on the journey ahead, but sickness or an injury could make survival ultimately impossible.

Mike found a sheltered spot downstream that he could use for cover while he cooked the rabbit and possibly camp out for the night. There was a wall of ice-covered rocks on three sides facing the stream that went back a few feet, and he felt confident he could defend this area if he needed to. It might have been a bear den at some point, because it looked like it had been partially dug out and there were bone remnants of some kind laying nearby. Nothing was occupying it now, or even recently, from what he could tell. It had a dank smell to it, but he would be out of the weather here. Mike knew he hadn't gotten very far from the crash this first day. The snowy and rocky terrain had made it difficult to move down the mountain very fast. Once things flattened out on the tundra he thought he'd get farther than a few miles a day, as long as it wasn't too wet and snowy. The thought brought him a little comfort.

Mike had never skinned a rabbit before, so he treated it like a deer, which seemed to work out.

"Not much meat on these things," he said, as he peeled off the hide.

The meager rations would have to do.

He thought about keeping the fluffy white pelt, but didn't know how to tan one without the proper items, like salt and chemicals. He did cut off the back feet for the boys and put them in his pocket. He remembered having a lucky rabbit's foot when he was a boy and thought it would be cool to give them one from an Alaska hare.

Mike collected as much wood and branches as he could find in the area. His growing pile of timber wouldn't last all night, but he thought it should make it most of the way through. He had fresh meat and his new camp would be warmer than the two previous nights he had spent in the plane.

While the rabbit was cooking, Mike moved some larger moss-covered rocks into a better defensive position in front of the opening in the rock wall. If he was attacked by anything, it would have no choice but to move through his choke-point and meet him head on.

Dinner cooked quickly. He sliced some meat and it wasn't pink, so he put it in his mouth. Without any seasoning, it wasn't great, but it was food.

"Tastes like chicken," he commented as he cut more off.

He had eaten many different wild animals, but none as gamey tasting as this. As he was eating the hare, Mike heard the faint sound of a plane engine. It was a whine at first, then got louder like it was cutting out and trying to throttle up. The sound soon went away completely. The fog was starting to dissipate, but night was falling again and he couldn't even see the tail or wing lights.

*This is a good sign,* he thought. *They're looking for us.*

Whether the plane was for him or not, it made him feel better to hear it. There were many villages on the peninsula scattered throughout the area to Bristol Bay and beyond, all the way to the Aleutian Islands.

The plane could be going anywhere, but the idea of a search plane sounded better than a commuter.

After choking down his dinner, Mike felt content with his stomach halfway full of something. The protein would give him strength, but he couldn't eat just meat.

He lit a cigarette from a branch that had been in the fire and enjoyed it after his small meal. He knew to ration them, to make them last, just like his food.

It was spring so berries wouldn't be available unless he wanted to search for some in the snow, still frozen from last year. He didn't know what plants were edible, even if he found any. He needed to be rescued, and soon, if he was going to make it.

"I'm going to read books on survival when I get back," Mike said to himself.

He drank a mouthful of water from his canteen to try and fill the void left in his stomach.

Mike built up the fire with most of the wood that was left. He finished smoking the cigarette, while the fire mesmerized him. The orange flames flickered, sending glowing embers sailing into the night sky. As the fire burned, it cast shadows on the walls of the rock enclosure and gave him a show.

Mike lay down on the cold, hard dirt floor and tried to get some sleep next to the warmth of the hot coals and burning sticks. He woke up a few times during the night, and put more wood on the fire until the stack was gone. He was fairly warm throughout the night, and knew he had it good compared to what lay ahead and what he had already been through.

Falling rocks woke him the next morning. He got up and stretched while yawning, and looked around to try to see what caused the rocks to move as he maneuvered slowly into the open. He scanned the area for a few minutes and decided it wasn't an animal that had made them fall, so he put the coals out and got ready to go.

Mike relieved himself, filled his canteen from the stream and started moving along it towards what he hoped was a river or a lake. He kept reassuring himself that there was something or someone at the end of the water. As he maneuvered around some rocks, he saw a raven sitting on the branch of a tree. The bird squawked at him and flew off.

The walking was getting easier like he had remembered from his previous trip as he transitioned from the rocky terrain to the tundra. There was daylight, but the sun couldn't be seen yet. There were patches of alders that he had to walk around from time to time, but it was getting better. He was very careful as he went through the bushes.

*At least there weren't any leaves this time of year to hide animals that could attack him,* he thought.

There were some wet spots where the snow had recently melted, and Mike avoided these as much as possible. The last thing he needed was to get wet and not be able to get dry quick enough before hypothermia set in. The surrounding mountains were still covered in snow and there were snow patches all around him, even at the lower elevations. It was melting with the warmer weather, but cold was a threat with the mercury still dipping below freezing at night.

The farther he went, Mike could see much more of the area in all directions, but the cloud cover was still very low.

He wondered whether a plane would be able to see him in these conditions. But, the sun was trying to burn through the clouds, and sometimes a few rays could be seen peeking through.

As he walked, Mike looked behind him and to his flanks to make sure nothing was tracking him. The mountains behind him to the north, from which he had come, got farther away as the day went on. He needed to get to some cover before nightfall, but he saw no trees in the distance.

Banks of thick mist were slowly rolling in front of him, making it harder to see very far. It wasn't just Mike's vision that was challenged by the featureless white. It brought danger and, even more perilous in his current situation, it brought doubt. Like those brief seconds when someone covers your eyes from behind, and says, "Guess who?" Mike didn't like surprises. Not that kind, and especially not the kind where he could potentially bump into a bear he didn't see coming. He hoped the fog would break soon.

He skirted around large pools of water that had collected from the melting snow. Some were bigger and looked like ponds. He hoped that some of these might have animals or birds in them that he could catch and eat, but so far he saw none.

The rolling lumpy tundra obscured views of the area until the terrain was right in front of him. Mike nearly missed two small lean-tos, hidden until he walked down a gravel embankment from a pad that had probably been used as an air strip for small planes. He could tell right away the shacks hadn't been occupied in a long time, but he needed a place to spend the night and these would work just fine.

Mike climbed a rickety observation tower by a defunct camp. Some of the wooden rungs were missing, so he was careful as he went up. The metal flagpole was rusted deeply, as were the nails holding the rotting wood together. From the higher vantage point he saw a line of trees barely visible in the distance over the low-lying blanket of mist on the ground, which he decided would be his waypoint the following day.

Mike took one more look all around before climbing back down and still struggled to recognize any of what he could see.

He carefully made his way inside the first lean-to with his spear leading the way. There was light shining through holes in the old wood and frayed tarp, so he let his eyes adjust once inside. It smelled of mildew as soon as he entered. He could start making out the mess inside and knew it would take a while to search the detritus to see if there was anything he could use. The wood was rotten and most anything made of metal was rusty. After searching, he decided it was all useless junk that was left inside, so he moved on. The second and larger lean-to had a little more to offer. He found a metal trashcan lid, which could double as an umbrella or a shield. There was about seven feet of small rope under some old blankets that had holes in them. There was an old wood stove with the door missing, and some broken stove pipe. It was better than nothing and would keep him warm for the night, so he reassembled it the best he could.

He felt like a king in a castle after the past couple of days. These conditions were the best he he'd had in what seemed like a very long time already. Shelter from the elements and predators was welcome for sure.

Mike moved as much of the old wood inside the lean-to in order to make a defensible position, keep the door shut and stay warmer and more protected. There was plenty of wood to burn for the night, and the holey blankets would keep him warmer than he had been on the mountain.

It had been three days since the crash, and Mike knew that hygiene would keep him healthier, but he dared not take off his clothes or boots to air them out. If a bear or wolves attacked, he'd be at a disadvantage. He was hungry but decided not to eat anything until morning when he would need more strength to walk again.

He stoked the fire with some of the boards and made the most of his nightly cigarette. After he was done with the smoke he eventually fell asleep on an old piece of plywood, head on the duffle bag, with his spear pointing outward and the trashcan lid beside him.

After what seemed like just a few minutes, Mike woke to the sound of sniffing and scratching at what was left of the door. He wiped his eyes with his sleeves and could see that hours had passed because the fire was burning out.

Whatever was outside would have a hard time getting in with the wood he had piled up against the old door. Mike quietly put more wood in the stove and tried to stay awake and alert, but he fell asleep anyway, fitful rest though it was.

Mike woke in the morning and the door was open. His mind reeled, searching for a clue to how all the wood had been moved out of the way, and without him hearing it. He felt some wind blowing on him from his right side. He looked over, and there was a big, black wolf snarling at him, its razor-sharp teeth glistening in the light of the fire. Thick drool was hanging out of both sides of its mouth. Mike's heart was pounding, as he sat there frozen in terror, knowing that this was his fate as the beast opened its mouth and bit Mike's face. He woke up and gasped, realizing it had only been a nightmare. One he hoped didn't happen again.

He took his gloves off, rubbed his face with his dirty hands and got up. It was morning. He had to keep going, even if it was just to the trees before nightfall. It was only another few miles in the grand scheme of things, but they represented one step closer to being back in the security of his home, where he could not only enjoy his recliner, watch football on TV and drink a beer again, but embrace his family and eat a real meal.

He moved the wood away from the door as quietly as possible and cautiously walked outside. There were wolf tracks all around the lean-to. The scratching and sniffing had been real. He had to wonder if they were the same pack from the mountain, and he had a nerve-racking feeling they were following him from the crash site. His head was swimming with thoughts of moving down a few notches on the food chain.

# Chapter Four: Survival

Mike devoured an energy bar for breakfast, drank a little water from his canteen and headed off toward his destination, keeping the stream in view. The mounds of tundra were pockmarked with holes, some with fresh dirt in front. These holes were from squirrel-like animals that reminded him of ground squirrels, just bigger, but they sat up like prairie dogs. The Natives called them "parka" because of the thick fur from which they make hats and coats. The little fur balls would run back and forth between the holes and were hard to shoot unless they were sitting still. On his last trip Mike had brought a.22 rifle with him after Ted told him how fun they were to shoot. If they weren't so hard to catch, he might have an unlimited food source. But there was no way he could get close enough to these little things. He needed a small-caliber gun to hunt them and that was somewhere on the mountain behind him, with all the rest of the supplies he needed.

A short distance away from the lean-to Mike stopped, and pulled the hood from his parka off, thinking he heard something. A faint buzz courted his attention as he scanned for a plane.

*Was it the same one?*

With the low clouds Mike didn't know where it was or where it was going, so he kept walking and looking up until he couldn't hear it any longer.

A *"squawk,"* which sounded more like "Mike," echoed from above.

Looking up, he could see a raven flying overhead.

"What do you want?" he questioned the bird as it squawked again, flew off into the distance and disappeared.

The trees seemed closer and Mike thought he could make out mountains beyond them to the southwest, but couldn't guess how far away they were, nor whether they were in the right direction. Hell, they might just be clouds. He couldn't be positive until he was closer.

The stream flowed to the left of the tree line, so Mike just kept following it. He had water and a path to follow that he hoped would lead him to people. He'd been walking all day and once again night was closing in.

His path leveled out just as the wind started to blow. He was glad to be around trees for cover. A natural wind block and firewood too.

He started looking for a place to spend the night in the dwindling light.

There were ptarmigan up in a tree and he knew if he wanted to get one that he would have to come up behind them very quietly or they would fly away. It wasn't hunting season for the bird, mainly white in color, but at this point he didn't care.

"They can fine me all they want if I make it back," he said to himself as he slowly made his way toward his quarry.

Mike skirted the spruce tree and came up slowly behind the birds. He would only be able to get one of them, but it was better than none. He took the sheath off the knife at the end of the pole and moved in for the kill. He raised the spear and moved the tip closer to the nearest bird. The small group started to make quiet cooing noises, talking to one another as if they knew something was wrong and were discussing flying away. He thrust the spear and missed. They flew off squawking as if taunting him.

More birds could be seen landing in the alders some distance away. Fatigue was setting in and Mike didn't relish the extra walking while trying to get a meal, especially with the blisters he could feel on his feet. After many failed attempts, success finally happened. One bird would satisfy him for the night.

Mike found a taller tree than the rest, one he could spend the night in. He attempted to make a fire close by so he could cook the bird. The wind made it difficult, so he used the trashcan lid as a break to get the grass and sticks started.

The night was getting cold with the wind blowing, and he didn't want to leave the warmth of the fire but knew he had to. The bird's breast meat wasn't very satisfying and looked much bigger whole. It wasn't entirely filling, either, given the long day of walking Mike had put in.

Before Mike put the fire out, he smoked a cigarette and counted them. "Only fourteen left," he said to himself.

A few were broken when he opened the pack, but he wasn't counting the partials yet, anyway. He felt his eye to check on the swelling. It was getting better, just like his arm, and he was glad for this. He put the fire out as reluctantly as the stub of his cigarette and looked up at the tree. This was the best choice he had.

Getting caught on the ground by a predator was not the way he wanted to go out.

Mike set the trashcan lid and the spear at the base of the tree and started climbing. About twenty feet up he secured himself with the small rope he had found in the lean-to. He wrapped the holey blankets around himself the best he could, rested on some branches and eventually fell asleep. He woke up many times and felt like he was falling. The wind cut through his cocoon, stealing what body heat he produced. The night was long and cold, and morning still came too quickly. Mike wasn't ready for the next leg of his journey, being so tired. He ate a few crackers, drank some water and continued on in the same direction. There were very few birds and no animals of any kind seen that day.

*There must be a storm blowing in,* he thought nervously. *A storm would cause all animals to find cover until the weather got better.*

Mike kept walking, following the tree line and stream the rest of the day. His ordeal was taking a toll both physically and emotionally. His feet were on fire, his back was aching and he was trying to focus on surviving. He decided that he had gone far enough and started looking around for a tree to sleep in.

The trees stopped just beyond where he was and there was more tundra in front of him. The stream kept on going, but why were all these trees here? Had he missed something? Was there a lake on the other side of the trees?

*All good questions,* he thought, but was it worth the extra time and distance to look, or should he just continue on with the original plan?

A possible plan B could wait until morning. He was more tired this night than he had been since the crash. He didn't even bother to build a fire or smoke, he just drank some water and struggled to climb the tree, weak from so much exercise and so little food. The strong winds would once again steal his warmth all night, making him more miserable.

The next morning, Mike woke up and realized with some relief that he had actually slept the whole night. The wind had died down and he saw sunshine peeking through the clouds. The rays continued to push though and made it look like a stairway to heaven. He then heard it again. It was the sound of a plane that had woke him up. He quickly untied the rope, climbed down the tree and moved out from the spruce canopy just in case the plane was overhead so it could see him. He stopped and intently listened. The sound of the engines slowly went away and he never saw the plane. His heart sank as he realized that he might never get to actually see the planes he kept hearing, and they wouldn't see him, either.

The wind had blown the fog and clouds away just enough that he could see a mountain range in front of him. Now he had a direction to travel. Today was the beginning of day six and his hunger was making its presence increasingly known. He had some food left, but felt it was important to ration it. The mountains looked a hundred miles away and he hoped that once he reached them, he wouldn't have to climb over them.

While getting ready to start his trek that morning, his stomach was gurgling. Looking around for a suitable place to relieve himself, Mike saw a deadfall with leaves surrounding it that would work nicely.

Feeling the need coming on more urgently now, he hurried to drop his pants, and did so just in time as an explosion could be felt and heard.

"Ahhh," he declared, feeling relief. "This can't be good."

After regaining his composure and getting dressed, he was ready to go.

Mike had made it many miles and there were no trees in sight. Night was slowly approaching and he didn't feel safe sleeping out on the tundra. He decided to push on through the night. His feet felt like they were on fire again and he knew he had blisters, but didn't dare stop or take his boots off. Once he found trees again, he would stop and sleep, even if it was bright daylight out. Every once in a while, he had that feeling that something was watching him, so the spear was kept very close to his body and he held on tight. He kept the revolver holstered. If he was knocked down, or fell then he might not be able to recover it. The wind had really died down and he was able to hear the stream and the occasional distant howl of a wolf and other sounds he didn't recognize.

The clouds had cleared to just some thin residual patches and the moonlight allowed him to see. Walking kept him warm and he was glad for it. The mountains were still in view, but still no trees. There were a few times that Mike felt as if he was falling asleep. He would stop and smack his face or splash some freezing water from the stream on it. He feared being caught out in the open, as he would be no match for the predators in this region.

Something caught Mike's eye from the west as he continued on. He stopped and kneeled to get a better view with the aid of the moonlight. A dark as midnight lone wolf, the Alpha, maybe, silhouetted against the top of a rise. It slowly made its way north and skirted the tree line before disappearing at a sprint. The hair on Mike's neck was standing at attention and he had a tingly feeling all over. Completely awake now and very alert, he knew he had to press on and find some tree's for safety.

More light could be seen on the horizon, and as Mike made his way through the rolling hills of the tundra, he could finally see a tree line in the far distance. He continued to plod along willing himself to make it there before he could rest. A smaller creek forked in front of him. He crossed it and continued following the larger stream.

Mike again was thankful that he had his boots on. His camp shoes would have fallen apart before he made it a few miles in these environmental conditions. These boots were hot on his feet as he walked and they were extra weight to muscle, but they kept them warm when he wasn't moving, too. The soles weren't the best for hiking, but they were completely waterproof and were rated to -40 degrees.

By what he guessed was mid-morning, Mike had finally made it to the tree line and was exhausted. He picked the closest tree that he thought was tall enough for safety and climbed it. He fell instantly asleep as soon as he roped himself in and closed his eyes.

He woke as the sun was going down to the sound of another plane. This time, the plane buzzed the tree tops. Mike untied himself as fast as he could and started to climb down. He lost his footing and fell. As soon as he hit the ground he woke up. It had been another dream. He'd woken up as he fell backward in his rope around the tree. It was completely dark and he wondered if there had been a plane at all.

He turned his cell phone on just to check the time, since the light on his watch was still not working. It was 3:37 a.m. He shut it off after looking at a picture of Rachel and the boys. He had to conserve the battery. If he got to a place with the smallest amount of service, he had to be able to call for help. Tears were welling up in his eyes as he thought about his family.

*Where did it all go wrong? All I do is provide for her and the boys,* Mike thought. *Why does that bitch treat me the way she does?*

He loved his wife, but the way she made him feel sometimes seemed wrong. Mike wiped his eyes with his dirty sleeve and tried to put it out of his mind. It would be morning soon, so he tried to go back to sleep, and finally did.

# Chapter Five: Tundra

Mike woke up in the tree to the sound of ptarmigan screeching at each other. The mating ritual of these birds annoyed him. He remembered the last time he was in the area during breeding season. He had wanted to put ear plugs in, but then he wouldn't have been able to hear anything approaching outside the tent. He could just go out and shoot them, but that wouldn't be right.

Ted's son, John, pointed out on the last trip, "They're just trying to live and mate."

So Mike put up with it and napped a little during the day to make up the sleep he lost at night. There were many documented cases of hunters, and other people on trips in the wilderness that had been attacked in their tents.

Mike vowed to John and Ted, "I'm not going to become a statistic."

He even slept with his revolver when he and his family were camping for the weekend, back when the boys were younger, the family hadn't gone camping in years.

Rachael thought camping was dirty, uncomfortable and inconvenient. She was scared to be in the wilderness away from modern conveniences and a sense of security, Mike reassured her that if something decided to enter the tent at night he had the protection of the handgun. He pointed out that it wasn't just for four-legged creatures either.

She reluctantly agreed and told him, "The boys have to sleep on the other side of the tent and you better have it with you during the day too."

She didn't want them getting a hold of the gun and shooting each other. Mike dreamed of teaching the boys to shoot and maybe even go on a hunting trip, but she would not even negotiate to ever allow this.

He untied himself from the tree as carefully and quietly as he could. Breakfast was on his mind now and he slowly got down out of the tree and looked for the closest source of the racket. The birds were around, he just needed one to land in a tree. Some of them finally did and he took the opportunity.

The sun was shining bright and was warming the morning. There was very little wind so he had to be quick. He stealthily made his way to a tree that had a few birds in it. He slowly moved the spear into position and quickly thrust it at a bird. He got one! Several birds flushed, but landed in a tree close to him, so he attempted to kill another. After a few hours of many attempts and following the birds around, Mike had two ptarmigan. He knew he was lucky and didn't expect this every time. He was soon gathering wood for a fire after his exhausting hunt.

Chasing the birds had taken time and had burned many calories, but he was practically drooling in prepping the best meal he had eaten in days. He cleaned the birds by the stream with his skinning knife. He sliced them open, taking out their innards' and peeling off the skin and feathers. He broke the wings and legs close to their bodies and cut the rest with his knife. Rinsing them one last time, he placed them on a rock while he cut some sticks to hold them over a fire.

Mike trudged back over to the stream to wash up while the birds were cooking. He saw himself in the clear water and was shocked. He was very dirty, and his beard was filling in.

"It hasn't been that long, has it?" he said to himself.

Pulling out his cell phone, he turned it on and looked at the date. It had been nine days since the crash. Where did the missing days go? He thought he had only been walking for seven days. He must have been on the mountain after the crash longer than he thought, or just lost track. He turned the phone off after a short look at Rachael and the boys and finished washing up.

Mike scanned the immediate area, seeing nothing out of the ordinary. He made his way back to the fire where he could smell the cooking flesh, which teased him with the aroma of chicken.

"*Squawk,*" came from over head.

The raven was back and was beginning to annoy him.

"Are you following me?" he asked the bird before it flew off, letting out another squawk.

Knowing that this food would only last so long, he tried to remember if there was anything else he could eat out, there besides berries that survived the winter under the spring's retreating blanket of snow. New ones wouldn't be ripe until the fall. He looked around and saw the buds on the end of a spruce tree branch.

*People make tea out of those, so they should be edible,* he thought. *Be nice if this stops my runs.*

Mike pulled one bud off a branch. He put it in his mouth, and began chewing, despite the bitterness of the bud.

"Tastes like a tree," he said, making a face.

His thoughts drifted to a night with Ted. They had gone to one of the local micro-brewery restaurants in town. One beer among several they had tasted, bragged about its spruce inspired flavor. He didn't like it then, and even in survival mode, didn't care for it now. He decided he would have to acquire the taste or, more likely, just deal with it. Mike gathered a handful of the tree buds and went back to the fire to eat.

The late morning meal consisted of water, bird and tree. He was careful to save some of the cooked meat for later. He cut off a part of his T-shirt to wrap the rest of the meat, and stuck it in his pocket. With a rock he scratched nine lines in the aluminum pole he used as a spear so he could keep better track of the days.

Mike put out the fire, gathered the rest of his belongings, looked around the area for a moment, then continued along down beside the stream toward the mountains.

Even though the day was clear, the surrounding mountains and the trees still didn't look familiar. He had hoped he would be able to recognize something he had seen on the last trip to the area. His original plan of following the stream would have to work for now. He would eventually come across something or someone, he hoped.

Before long, his back was itching something fierce. He found a stick to scratch with, but it didn't get all the spots enough to satisfy him. Mike noticed some rub marks on a nearby tree and remembered how his boys had laughed at a bear while at the San Diego Zoo. The bear was backed up against a tree in his habitat and was rubbing his back all over it. Mike decided to try this technique, and after hitting all of the spots on a tree, he tossed the stick.

"I'm going to have to remember that," he told himself.

Mike walked for two more days and many more miles with fairly good weather and no more predator sightings. The ground squirrels were all over the place, but he still had no way of hunting them. Sometimes he would see a very large hole cut out of a bank where he knew the small animals lived. It was probably dug by a bear, or a coyote, or maybe a wolf trying to get to them.

He knew there are many animals that survive year-round on the tundra. He couldn't forget about the red foxes and thick, muscular wolverines that were out there, too.

The stream seemed endless as he traveled along. The mountains to the east were getting closer, and Mike kept wondering if he would have to cross over them before he got to the ocean. The stream could just skirt the mountains before empting into a lake or river, for all he knew at this point. The wind was picking up again and clouds were moving in. The weather in this area could change drastically at any moment, and he had to deal with it the best he could. Mike knew that this probably meant rain and getting wet. The trash can lid would only keep him so dry, and it would be hard to keep himself covered all night in a tree. The inevitable rain started later that day.

Most of his clothing was waterproof, or at least water resistant. The Gore-Tex would dry quickly if water did soak through, but if he caught a cold, his situation could still go downhill fast. Staying dry was a priority, even if it slowed his pace.

Not much shelter could be found in the trees. The branches only partially blocked the drops of water working to sabotage him. The harsh winters in this area stunted the grown of vegetation. Much of Alaska's environment is shaped by the extreme weather.

He would have better luck staying dry on the ground with a fire, but was afraid it might attract predators. Mike told himself that the rain would eventually stop and he could dry off when it did. And it did for a while, but started back up again. He continued on in a new level of damp, chilly misery, which only slowed his pace.

After days of gray skies and on-and-off rain, birds started chirping in the trees. It didn't do much to improve his mood, and Mike wallowed in thoughts about his disintegrating family. He knew he hadn't become the man Rachael thought he would be. Once he lost the football scholarship and attended community college for a business degree, the relationship wasn't the same. He had worked his way up to assistant manager and then store manager at the grocery store, but he still felt like he had given up. Even Mike didn't feel good about his life.

He found himself asking Rachael for permission to go play poker at Eric's house with the guys, or to buy something over a hundred dollars, even though he was the one working and supporting the family. His boys had better and more-expensive phones than he did. He constantly felt sub-par, emasculated, and tried to understand how he let it all get out of hand. Going on hunting or business trips was what kept him sane. The time away let him feel like himself again and forget about the meaninglessness his life had become.

He and Rachael very rarely had sex anymore, and when they did, it was boring and unfulfilling. An act he almost felt like he was obligated to perform. It wasn't supposed to be that way. It didn't used to be.

"Things will be different this time," Mike vowed "When I get back, I will be the man I really am."

The farther he walked, the worse the blisters on his feet got, as was the chafing on his inner thighs and ass cheeks. He didn't have to look at any of it to know how bad it was, he could feel it. The jeans he was wearing under the waterproof pants were not the best to be wearing for all the walking he was doing. The sweat pants he would normally have on under the waterproof outer layer would allow for less-restricted movement.

"At least my other injuries have healed pretty well," said Mike, thinking of his eye and arm. "Have to stay positive, buddy."

The mountains to the east appeared were closer and looking taller too. The flat tundra gradually became rolling hills, and patches of spruce trees and alders were getting thicker. One afternoon, Mike saw a lone bear a few miles away on a rise. It was walking along the top of a small hill and obviously had no sense of his presence. The bear was far enough away that he couldn't determine its species. Mike figured he was down-wind, and that was exactly where he wanted to remain. If the animal could smell him, then it might decide to move his way to investigate.

He continued to the next patch of trees as the day passed and the sun went down.

Being alone in the woods and not knowing if what you're doing is right is mentally exhausting. Should he have stayed close to the crash site? How long would it have been before help, or more danger, came? Was the emergency beacon even working? All of these concerns weighed heavily on Mike's mind. He had survived this long, but today his mind was filling with doubt.

Being emotionally alone was something Mike was used to, but there were usually other people around.

*How much longer could he do this?*

Did he miss the comfort of just knowing others were around, or was it that he needed them there?

"Many other people have done what I'm doing and not gone crazy," he said to himself.

Then, "This is bad, I'm talking to myself again."

Mike struggled to keep moving, worried that if he didn't find help soon, that he would lose it completely.

The thought of the life he left back in the "real world" motivated each foot forward. He hurt all over his body, but knew he needed to go on for himself, for his boys. He wasn't ready to not be in their lives.

The nights were cold and lonely. The thought of predators sneaking up on him as he walked along the tundra was no comfort.

The occasional fox, wolverine or wolf could be seen in the distance, and occasionally close up. Mike found himself looking at tracks trying to figure out what they were. The occasional pile of some kind of animal droppings was seen, but none that looked too fresh. The larger ones were from bears, and he didn't like seeing them.

"What the hell am I doing? I don't know what these belong to," he said loudly one day while looking at more tracks.

He heard what he guessed was a coyote calling after him. "You tell her buddy," he mumbled, then drank from his canteen.

His mind meandered like the stream he followed. Work, his home life, his poor aunt, how would he tell her about her husband's death when he got back? If he got back.

"No, when I get back," he confirmed to himself.

So many nights around the fire cooking birds or just warming up, he smoked a cigarette and thought how good a beer and pizza would taste. He thought of these things as hungrily as a fifteen-year-old boy looking at porn for the first time.

But those were inefficient distractions from pondering his life and what he'd accomplished up to this point.

"Not much," he concluded.

He was supposed to be playing in the NFL by now, living in a mansion and driving a flashy sports car with all the bells and whistles. There wasn't much use in dwelling on what could have been. He was in this situation now and life was what it was back home.

"But, I can make some changes," he vowed. "And I will."

Mike continued walking along the stream as the light on the horizon continued to fade and he seemed to be walking into nothingness.

# Chapter Six: Cabin in the Woods

It was getting darker when Mike saw the lake in front of him. The stream he'd been following from the mountain where they crashed finally connected with a body of water. He couldn't see much of it in the dim light, but was hopeful it was large enough that there might be people living near it.

And as hungry as he was, he was particularly hopeful there were fish in it.

"But how the hell am I going to catch them?" he wondered out loud.

He would try to figure something out in the morning, so he looked around for a suitable tree and started climbing. Mike was positioning the trash can lid on branches above him to keep rain off. He had just got settled when he saw something on the other side of the lake. It looked like a house, but he wondered if he was just seeing things in the fading light. He got down from the tree and skirted the left shore of the lake. He didn't want to cross the deep stream, but he might have to unless he could find a place to cross where he wouldn't get wet.

He backtracked upstream until he found the cluster of fallen alders that crossed the stream over which he could climb. If what he spied from the tree didn't turn out to be anything, he would just climb another tree for the night.

Mike kept walking in the rain as the light continued to fade. He had to see what was there. Sure enough, it was a small cabin tucked away in the trees with a small dock by last year's lily pads on the edge of the lake. There were no lights on, and no float plane at the dock, so he felt sure no one was home. More of the lake was visible now and he could tell that it was pretty large. In the twilight it was hard to make out any details, but this was so much better than a tree, and it didn't matter if it was run down or not. He smiled approaching the structure.

"There really is light at the end of the tunnel."

He pulled the flashlight out of the small duffle and turned it on. It was almost dead, but bright enough for him to see inside. Mike put down his spear and trash can lid and pulled his revolver out of its holster.

With the flashlight on, he made his way to the door. It had a padlock on it, so he went back to get the spear. Mike bent the latch and broke it off with the pole, allowing him to enter the small cabin. He smelled a dank odor, like rotting wood. Putting the spear down and pointing the revolver forward again, he found an oil lantern and some matches just as the flashlight dimmed and became a useless yellow glow. He lit a match and lit the wick. The room came to life with light and he could see everything laid out in front of him.

The whole thing appeared to have been constructed of scrap that must have been flown over on numerous occasions. Mike closed the door and saw a board against the wall he could use to secure the door with hanging hooks on both sides. There was a belly-stove made of thick iron in the rear left corner and some wood stacked by it, along with scraps of paper. Mike opened the doors to the stove to make a fire. After getting it going, he continued to look around. This was definitely a hunting cabin with moose and caribou antlers adorning the walls, and it hadn't been used in at least a season, by the looks of it.

The wooden cots had foam on them, but no bedding. There was a loft above, so Mike climbed the ladder with the lantern to look. There were two more beds and nothing else, so he climbed back down.

*Everything they need must be brought out when they fly out,* Mike thought disappointedly.

The door was secure and the fire was getting the small cabin warm, so Mike took his boots off and let his feet breathe. This felt so good he decided to take his socks and most of the rest of his clothes off. Carefully peeling off the socks, that had been stuck to his badly hurting feet, he could see blood stains and chunks of skin in them from broken blisters. His feet had brought him pain for many days. This was the perfect opportunity to let them heal before continuing on. He and his clothes really made the small cabin stink as it got warmer with the fire.

"It must really be bad when you can smell yourself," he said, with both amusement and disgust.

He shrugged his shoulders and didn't care that he smelled so bad he considered himself in heaven now. He ate the last bites of ptarmigan and spruce buds in his pocket, lit a cigarette and leaned back in a folding chair he found in a corner. The tobacco made the cabin smell a little better, he thought. More content than he had been in days, he moved over to relax and fell instantly asleep on the foam on the closest bed to the fire after finishing his cigarette.

Mike woke up hours later and was cold. The fire had burned down to coals, so he got up and put more wood in the stove and put the lantern out. It was still dark out, so he covered up with his holey blankets that had dried by the fire and went back to sleep.

Mike slept a long time, which was desperately needed. He woke up and it was bright daylight out, but still raining. He put more wood in the fire and decided to take advantage of the weather. He had had the same clothes on for almost two weeks. Even though he had no soap, he went out to wash his clothes in the lake, looking around the area outside the cabin as he walked out to make sure that he would be alright out there in just his skivvies.

He could see the whole structure now that it was daylight. It was built between a few large trees which gave it cover from the weather. Most of it was constructed of small pieces of plywood, just like the inside. Some trees had been used in the construction, too, giving it stability.

Mike walked out to the little dock and piled up all of his clothes and blankets. He scrubbed one piece at a time with a rock and took them back into the cabin to hang up and dry by the fire, then went back out to jump in the lake to wash himself off. The part of the lake he washed his clothes in looked muddy compared to the rest and Mike started to laugh as he jumped in. The water was very cold, so he didn't spend much time in it. He got out and ran into the cabin to warm up.

The clothes and blankets didn't take long to dry with the fire going, so Mike started getting dressed as soon as he could. He had seen a small out building and wanted to go check it out. The rain had stopped by the time all his clothes dried. His feet were swollen now that he had taken his boots off, and putting them back on was painful indeed. After screaming a little, he got them back on. His feet were tender, but he couldn't walk very far without the boots.

Mike slowly made his way out to the small building to see what he could find. This was locked up, too, which he hoped meant that there was something good in it. He pried the hinges open on one door and went inside with the lantern. He found some fishing poles and a small raft with a foot pump. There was an axe and a few shovels inside, too. It would be dark soon, so Mike figured he would try and catch some fish in the morning. After turning around to go back to the cabin, he noticed an outhouse. Curiosity got the better of him, since he had been wiping with leaves for weeks, a messy task since he had the runs every time he defecated. Mike opened the door and lo and behold, there was a partial roll of toilet paper. Smiling, he knew what he would be enjoying the next time he felt the urge. Closing the door to the throne room, he went back inside for the night.

He was hungry, but this was no different than most nights he spent since the crash. He relaxed by the fire and spent the evening pumping up the raft and getting a fishing pole ready.

*Now I just need to figure out how to use a fly rod,* he thought.

He put more wood in the stove, noticing he would have to bring more in from outside in the morning. There were a lot of logs cut up into rounds on the side of the cabin, they would just have to be split. He made sure the door was locked, then turned the lantern off and went to sleep in the wooden cot.

The next morning, Mike was eager to catch some fish. It was drizzling and gray, but he had to get some food, and he had a warm place to dry off when he was done.

The raft was still inflated, but decided to try from the dock first. There were a few fish jumping, making things look promising. He let out some line and whipped the fly pole back and forth and finally let the small, purple-and-red fly lay on the water. He tried this several times, but no fish bit.

An eagle landed with a large splash on the other side of the lake and, flapping its massive wings came back up with a fish in its talons.

"Show off," he yelled.

Mike decided to find some worms or slugs and try the old-fashioned way. After getting some plump worms and a few slimy slugs from under some old logs and rocks, he took the raft out and moved toward some rotten lily pads in the middle where bigger fish might be. He baited the hook on the line and lowered it into the water with a rock tied to the line as a weight. Almost instantly he had a fish on and it was fighting. He brought up a nice Dolly Varden, and just as he was about to pull it in, the fish fell off the line.

The makeshift weights didn't fall off every time, but they did need to be replaced quite often. Over the course of a few hours, he got several bites before he ran out of bait and rocks. But he landed two in the raft, which lifted his spirits, He even felt hopeful and excited for the next day.

He rowed back to the dock with a small paddle to clean the fish. Never actually catching these fish before, he marveled at the green on their back and sides, which turned white toward the belly. There were yellow and light pink spots scattered about the body, too. The fins were plain, but not transparent, he noticed. He sliced them open with his knife, took out the guts and cut the heads and tails off.

After he was done, he went inside to eat and relax. There were frying pans on the shelves, but nothing to put in them, like oil, so Mike wrapped the fish in old leaves he found outside and rinsed off in the lake before putting them in the pan. This helped to not burn the fish so bad. He added water, also to help cook the fish, and with the skin still on, this helped, as well. He had gotten used to no seasoning, but still fantasized about it on the meat.

The next day while fishing, Mike heard squirrels chattering at each other and decided to go hunting after fishing. He had a hard time getting the tree rodents with his feet hurting so much. He would make do with what he could catch and knew he needed to heal.

On his way back to the cabin a squirrel was chattering at him and ran up the nearest tree. He thrust the spear at it but missed, like he had with the others, as the bushy-tailed creature ran farther up and kept chattering, to Mike's disappointment.

This daily routine lasted about a week before he decided to continue his journey. He had hoped that while he was there hunters might land on the lake, but no one came. He figured that this game unit must not be in the spring rotation for brown bear hunting. He was safe and warm here on the lake, but badly wanted to get home. Mike knew he was still losing weight. Even with his new and abundant source of protein, it wasn't enough nourishment, but he had been eating some food daily and getting plenty of rest, so he hoped he would have enough strength to walk a longer distance. His feet were healthy again and the recovered blisters turned to calluses.

A rain storm lasting two days had finally subsided, so he planned on leaving with the good weather. He left a note for the owner of the cabin on the table with charcoal, saying who he was, thanking him and pointing the direction he was headed. He locked the shed and the cabin back up the best he could with logs against the doors and felt as ready as he could be.

The lake was much larger than he had thought and opened up into a very large body of water as he made his way along it. Since coming across the cabin he hadn't ventured very far, and besides his current predicament, enjoyed the serenity of his surroundings.

Hearing squawking overhead for the first time in over a week, Mike looked up to see a raven.

"Are you the same one?" he asked the bird. "What are you doing?"

This was very curious and was on his mind since seeing the raven the first time. Could it be the same one, and if so, why was it following him? He had only seen one of the birds at a time, never in pairs or more, and thought this odd, too.

He continued on for another two days and finally saw the end of the lake. Mike picked the stream up at the west shoreline of the water. Most of the walking was done on tundra and wasn't too bad.

As the lake emptied back out into a stream, he continued on with his plan to get to the coast and hopefully run into civilization, along the way.

The stream continued skirting the woods and moved out into the tundra and gravel pads, meandering lazily, to its destination. Mike figured that the gravel deposits in many of the areas were left from a glacier. The weather looked as if it would stay good for a while which suited him just fine. The mountains continued to get closer on all sides as he moved forward, and he knew he would reach them soon. He hoped the stream cut through the tall peaks and he wouldn't have to climb over them.

He knew that the cooked fish and birds he packed would last him about a week with rationing, so he wouldn't pass up an opportunity to catch any other game.

Mike tried to focus on survival, but his mind wandered to his life back home.

"They might think I'm dead," he said, and stopped for a moment. "If a search team finds the crash and I'm not there, will they keep looking for me? My god, what have I done? They will bury an empty coffin and move on. How long will she wait? I was only supposed to be gone for a week."

Would he see Rachel again? She was what kept him going, even though they weren't on the best of terms, along with the twins, too. Jim and Jack would be starting spring baseball soon and he would be missing it.

The boys were named after Jack Daniels and Jim Beam, two of Mike's favorite drinks when he wasn't drinking beer, and sometimes when he was. Rachel didn't want to name them after liquor at first, but Mike had talked her into it. It would be a great conversation piece, he told her. She finally relented, but said, the next children they had would be named by her and he agreed.

Years passed after the boys had been born and they were twelve now. He wondered if they would have any more kids or if they would even stay together.

Rachael had gotten pregnant their senior year in high school. With the college football scholarship Mike had as an all-star quarterback, he figured he would be able to provide for all of them, that is until he got hit hard from the side on a blitz and slipped two disks his back. During the second to last game of the season, the state championship, Mike was hit really hard by two players on the opposing team. His back had been hurt so bad that he was told by doctors he would never play another game.

Marrying one of the hottest girls in school was a good and bad thing. She was smart and beautiful, but this was also her downfall or Mike's. He was always wary of other guys no matter how confident he was in their relationship. His jealously seemed to be a game for her and he struggled to hide how bad this hurt.

The next few days went pretty well considering Mike still didn't know where he was. There continued to be more bear signs, and this was a concern. Seeing prints in the mud from different animals was one thing, but claw marks on trees and bear scat was alarming.

Not being an expert, however, he didn't really know how old any of it was.

Endless patches of trees and rocky outcroppings became Mike's new habitat as he pressed on.

"Same thing, different day," said Mike, sarcastically. "At least the lake brought a little excitement to the days."

Small bodies of water and clusters of alders made things very slow going again as he had to navigate around them. It seemed as if he was going uphill sometimes, which seemed strange.

"It's a good thing I'm in shape," he commented as he walked.

Going to the gym, lifting weights and exercising was something he always did, whenever he found time. The workout regime was even more intense before he went on the hunt in order to make sure he was in good enough shape to pack in, and out, of the mountains.

He continued to follow the stream, so he couldn't possibly be gaining altitude. He now stopped from time to time and climbed a tree to scan the area to find the best way through the mess in front of him. After climbing down from a tree, Mike headed to a game trail he spied. It went through what looked like a sparse cluster of spruce and alders.

With the new obstacles, the journey would take longer and Mike would need more food, and so far he wasn't finding much after leaving the lake. He had considered going back many times since he had left, but knew this was the best thing he could do.

The weather was still good, the only thing going in his favor. He could feel blisters starting to form on both feet again as he kept pushing forward and didn't like that at all. Blisters brought pain that slowed him, and a greater chance of infection. Chafing started on the insides of his thighs again, just like before. There was nothing that could be done about it except stop walking and he couldn't do that. He was starting to get sores in his mouth, too, and he figured it was from his lack of fruit and proper nutrition. The mountains were looming in the foreground to the east and he continued to wonder what lay ahead.

As he picked his way along the path, he suddenly felt uneasy. He looked around the area and slowly moved forward. In a small clearing, he saw a moose calf lying on the ground. The animal wasn't moving and was steaming, with blood by its head.

"A fresh kill!" he said softly to himself. Mike quickly drew his pistol and tucked the spear up under his left armpit, scanning the area.

# Chapter Seven:
# Confrontation

Something was out there, but what?

"More damn wolves or a bear this time?" Mike asked himself, softly.

He slowly backed up into a tree branch. He spun around, wanting to yell, but holding back. Seeing it was only a branch after fear shot down his spine, he turned back, and saw her as she slowly moved into view. A very large, majestic and very upset brown bear sow, right in front of him. She stood up and pierced the quiet morning, with a bellowing roar. Showing her razor sharp teeth, Mike's heart was pounding like a jack hammer in his chest. He continued to slowly back up and put a tree between him and the bear for some sort of protection should she decide to attack. She dropped back to the ground with a thud, seeming to shake the ground and charged forward. She stopped about ten feet from Mike and stomped her front paws on the ground, huge claws tearing into the earth, and roared again.

The bear was massive with small ears, meaning she was old, but this meant she had experience. A chunk of fur was missing from her front right leg, lost during one of many fights, no doubt. Other than the missing fur, she had a nice, semi blonde coat on.

Snapping back to reality, Mike realized he had his finger on the trigger and almost fired his revolver, but didn't. At that moment, encountering such a large bruin, he felt like David facing Goliath.

"What do you want?" Mike roared back, not wanting to show his fear and hoping that it worked.

He caught a glimpse of movement to his left, and saw why she was so angry. Her cub was so close to him that he could almost pet the small animal, and he was close to their kill at the same time.

The furry little ball next to him was making a whining noise now, like a baby would, and then suddenly started screaming over and over.

"I'm sorry," said Mike. "I didn't know. I'm going to find another way through and leave you two alone."

This got the sow's attention again and she still looked pissed off, snorting and clacking her jaws while moving toward her cub.

He continued to slowly back away, keeping his eye on the bears the whole time. The sow moved between Mike and her cub. They watched him leave and the sow calmed down. Then they went back to eating their meal, which was what they really wanted to do. Mike almost salivated while thinking of a lost chance to eat moose meat, but wasn't interested in the fight to attain it. He couldn't live with himself if he killed the sow and cub. They were just trying to survive, like him. He wasn't completely starving yet, but knew he would need some more food soon.

Mike decided to climb a tree some distance away from the bears to get his bearings after going off track. After getting high enough to see the stream again, he made his way back down to continue on.

Moving so far out of his intended path took the rest of the day. Hoping to find game on the path had worked, but not the way he had intended. He could stop where he was, or keep going across the next clearing. Getting as far away from the bears as he could was the best choice, considering he didn't know where their den was, either. They could eat the small moose in no time and be looking for more food soon. The sow was hungry from sleeping all winter and the cub was growing. They would be eating whatever they could find at this point like many predators in the springtime. He had no interest in becoming their meal.

Mike was almost to the next clearing and decided not to waste time by climbing a tree to look for a good route.

*I just need to cross this and get off the ground for the night*, he thought.

The clearing was larger than Mike had guessed while scanning it from the tree-line. It was getting close to dark, but he decided to cross to the other side anyway. The light was fading on the horizon as he was crossing the open area between the patches of trees.

The moonlight helped as it got darker, but it was still getting harder to see right in front of him. The hair on Mike's neck was standing at attention the farther he got out into the open. He felt as if he had dozens of eyes on him from every direction. He moved at a faster pace. A lone wolf's howl was heard too close for his liking. Mike stopped to listen, and all he could hear was his heart pounding in his ears as a bead of sweat rolled down his left cheek.

# Chapter Eight:
# Unbelievable

Between the heart beats in his ears, Mike heard footfalls on the tundra and franticly started looking around. Flashes of something moving on the horizon could be seen in the fading light. Fear was overcoming him as he anticipated something about to happen.

All of a sudden, seemingly out of nowhere, he was knocked down with a frontal attack and had the powerful jaws of the biggest wolf he had ever seen right in his face. Its eyes were glowing in the moonlight, which made it look even more menacing. Luckily, the aluminum rod he was using as a spear and walking stick had moved in front of him as he fell, and the wolf had it between its jaws.

Growling and snapping on the pole, the beast tried to reposition for another strike. The animal's large paws and claws were digging into Mike as they wrestled. Struggling, but finally pushing the pole off with his left hand, Mike pulled his revolver out of its holster and shot the beast in the head. Warm blood and brain matter sprayed everywhere and he felt its wetness on his face. The sound was deafening so close to his head. The monster fell on top of him and he had to crawl out from under it.

He stayed down on one knee and looked toward the horizon. The wolf pack could be seen circling around him in the faint light. He knew he wouldn't get lucky again. This initial wolf was testing his defenses. The pack would gang up on him, and without light to shine on the area he wouldn't know where they were coming from. He had to do something, and quick.

Mike bolted into action. He moved the spear tight in front of him to block anymore frontal advances, while leaving his back exposed. He pulled out the few matches he had left. The grass around him was dry, but was it dry enough? He lit a match and pulled some grass over the flame. It started to spread but then slowly died out.

His vision was gone completely now, until he lit the second match. This time, the grass caught and continued to slowly spread. The flames got bigger and he made his way toward the trees on the other side of the clearing, following the fire. Only some of the small trees caught fire, but didn't continue to spread, as some were still too wet. Most of the trees in this area were far enough apart that the flames hopefully wouldn't get too big.

Mike quickly climbed the nearest large tree. After getting halfway up, he stopped and roped off. The fire didn't continue burning, and Mike was glad for this. He didn't want to burn down the forest, but he needed to get away from the wolves.

The fire continued to die down and the wolves were nowhere to be seen or heard for some time. He vigilantly watched the area as the flickering light succumbed to darkness again. Mike only slept a little that night. He could hear the wolves howling from different areas early in the morning as if they were plotting another attack.

As light could finally be seen on the horizon, he saw that a large portion of the clearing was burned and a few trees on each side had. The wolf he killed lay in the middle of the burned area.

Recounting what had happened the day before, Mike's head was swimming. Being tired didn't help matters, but continuing on was the only choice.

A squirrel chattering close by caught his attention.

"What the hell else can happen?" Mike said softly as he rubbed his weary eyes.

Sitting in his makeshift cradle, he waited for more light to brighten his surroundings before getting down. While eating some of the little food he had left, he wished he had some paper and a pen to write down his experiences on his journey. Not that he would forget anything that had happened, but it would be nice to put it all down while it was still fresh in his mind.

Finally satisfied with how bright it was and with the sun coming up on the horizon, Mike untied the rope and got ready to get off his perch. More squirrel chatter was heard as he was doing this and he wondered what might be exiting them.

# Chapter Nine: Relentless

He made his way down the tree. As he reached the bottom, a wolf jumped up at him, growling and snapping. It seemed to come out of nowhere. He thrust the spear into it as it jumped up, and the animal took the spear with it as it fell back to the ground. He climbed back up a few feet as two more wolves approached, snarling and snapping their jaws. The animals were slowly circling the tree. Mike pulled his revolver out and aimed carefully at one of them. His bullet made contact and the wolf fell to the ground. It was still alive, trying to crawl away. The other one ran off before he could shoot it. Hanging on to a branch and stepping on another, Mike took the two empty cases out of the cylinder and put two live ones in so he had six in the gun again. He was now down to seven rounds total. Looking around, he slowly climbed out of the tree and walked over to the wolf with the spear in it. He pulled it out and walked over to finish off the one he had shot. Mike thrust the spear into the very large canine as it was moving away slowly, delivering a quicker death. He looked around the area again to make sure there weren't any more wolves. They were still out there, watching him he could sense this. He stood back and couldn't believe the size of these monsters.

Mike kicked the nearest one out of frustration, yelled, "You've got to be kidding me! What did I do to deserve this?"

He pulled his cell phone out of his pocket and turned it on for a quick picture. The animals were enormous and no one would believe him. After taking two pictures, he turned the phone back off and continued back on his way toward the mountains along the stream, frequently scanning all around and looking behind. Every once in a while, he would stop and listen for a few minutes, all the while looking in every direction for the wolves.

Was his luck running out? Mike's fears continually resurfaced as he made his way along the stream that morning. The last twelve hours had been heart stopping. How unlucky could he be encountering bears and wolves in the same day? He contemplated again if he should have just stayed back at the cabin. Someone was bound to show up for a hunt or to check on their lease, but the question was, when? If he waited until fall, and no one showed up then he would have a dilemma. If he continued in the same direction with the mountains to the east and eventually hit the coast late in the year, would he find help before winter? It was too much of a risk. Just being out on the tundra with inappropriate gear and a serious lack of groceries to sustain him was risk enough.

The days were slowly getting longer with daylight, but Mike was losing energy earlier every day. Food was still very scarce and he knew he was losing weight fast. The closer he got to the mountains, the colder the nights became. This didn't help, either.

One morning after climbing out of the tree he had slept in, Mike made his way down to the stream to splash cold water on his face and wake up. As he knelt down, he heard what sounded like thunder and splashing just upstream from where he was. The ground was shaking like an earthquake. Mike slowly and cautiously crept in the direction of the commotion. He saw a few caribou running frantically through the stream from one side to the other. He climbed the nearest tree to, not only get out of the way, but to get a better view of the situation.

What was now visible was truly amazing.

# Chapter Ten: The Herd

He could see an entire herd of them running toward the area he was in. As they got closer the tree started shaking and everything got very loud, like thunder on a stormy night. The tree he was in and those around it were repeatedly being hit by the animals, and his was swaying as if blown by a strong wind. He held the tree in a death grip and watched the unbelievable sight until the last of the caribou crossed the stream and the cloud of dust started settling. Mike could see now what had caused the frenzy. Not far away, wolves were feasting on a few young caribou they had caught. They were about forty feet away and focusing on the meal, so Mike took advantage of the situation. He pulled his revolver out of its holster, carefully aimed at what he thought was the Alpha and pulled the trigger. The gigantic black wolf yelped and fell instantly when hit by the bullet. It tried to get back up, but couldn't. The other wolves ran away when the shot was fired. Mike climbed down the tree and started walking carefully through the swath that had been cut by the caribou herd. With the food that the wolves had on the other side of the stream, Mike was confident they wouldn't follow him, so he decided to walk along the damaged area for a while, keeping the stream in sight. Hoping the herd hadn't gone too far, he thought this might be the opportunity he desperately needed to get a large amount of meat. All he needed was to be able to get one small caribou in order to attain the strength to carry on.

As he walked along the trampled earth, he heard what sounded like whining a few hundred yards away from where he had started. He stopped to listen and heard it again. He pulled out his revolver and followed the sound. Soon he came across a wounded caribou. The animal had broken its right front leg and was having a hard time getting up. This was an even better opportunity than he had hoped for and quickly thrust his spear into the hurt caribou's neck.

He was only a few hundred yards away from the wolf pack and their kill, but he knew this might be the last chance like this. Mike quickly untied the skinning knife from the pole and bled the animal. The meat would taste very gamey after it had been running with so much adrenaline and its hurt leg, but Mike had to get the protein. This would be like thirty birds worth of meat all at once, probably more. Bleeding it should help the taste. Mike decided to only take one back quarter and the back strap. He had killed and skinned many deer from the time he was a kid, so it wouldn't take long to salvage these parts of the animal and get out of the area. He took the skinned meat and attached his small rope to it. He threw it over his back and proceeded to get as far away as he could.

With the wolves and the caribou herd that morning taking up so much time, Mike had only been able to walk a few miles that afternoon before deciding he should call it quits for the day. The sun was going down and he knew he only had a short time to stop, hang the quarter and cook the back strap before he would have to climb a tree for the night.

With a dwindling supply of matches, Mike lit another fire to cook the meat. He ate some spruce branch ends while he waited for the meat to cook on the rock he had positioned over the flames. The caribou quarter would only last him so long before spoiling, so he would have to eat his fill every day before it went bad.

The meat was cooked, but didn't taste the best. It was better than nothing and he would choke it down to stay alive. After eating as much as he could stomach, Mike opened the pack of cigarettes and couldn't believe he was down to five of them. He had gone a few nights without smoking to make them last longer.

*A few more days and it will be quitting time again,* he thought.

The fire was going out and he was getting tired. After lighting the cigarette, he relaxed for a few minutes before he put it out completely and climbed the tree behind him. He secured the caribou in an adjacent tree, climbed another and tried to get some sleep.

His friendly raven was back in the morning and the squawking woke him as if it was saying it was time to get up.

"Okay, okay, I hear you, man," said Mike, a little annoyed.

He made his way down the tree and the raven flew off. He stretched and yawned while looking up at the caribou quarter, and saw something moving next to it, and then heard it.

"Hoo," was the sound of an owl.

"Oh no, you don't," said Mike to the bird as he climbed the tree thinking, it was going after his meat.

The owl spread its wings and flew away. Mike couldn't believe how big it was. Its wingspan was the size of a large model plane.

"Whoa," he said, as it flew right by him.

He got the quarter down from the tree and got ready for the day.

# Chapter Eleven: Accident

The days passed without any more animals trying to kill him and Mike was able to fall into a sort of rhythm with his journey. The caribou supply, his main sustenance for a few days, was almost gone now and he would soon be back to hunting birds, which were scarce. He slowly made his way across the tundra, closing in on the mountains, still hoping he could find a way through to the coast without much trouble. He didn't recognize any landmarks and wondered again how far off course Ted had flown them in the fog. The weather looked as if it could get bad again. The wind continued to pick up in the late afternoon one day and didn't appear to look like it would stop or even slow down. Mike wanted to climb a tree for safety, but was afraid it could blow down in the night with the extra weight from him in it. He searched for an alternate place to hole up and possibly fortify. Just before dark, he found a few newly fallen trees that had crossed each other on the ground and provided a natural barrier into which he could crawl. Rain still threatened, but was hesitating, however he wasn't going to count on his luck to hold. Luck hadn't been on his side since he got in the airplane to go on this trip. He pointed the spear outward from his small deadfall fortress and eventually fell asleep.

The night was cold and Mike could tell that he was in a large valley as clouds sunk low around him at night, but cleared off in the morning. Many old trees littered the ground and large rocks emphasized the change ahead. He noticed whole sections of mountainside ripped out by an avalanche or landslide.

"Maybe the volcano that had erupted in 1989," Mike reflected.

He continued to make his way through the trees and knew that the natural maze would take him longer to negotiate.

"Redoubt," Mike remembered. "The volcano was Mt. Redoubt."

The volcano was a landmark of the western Interior and could be seen for a hundred miles on a clear day from many areas. The mountain had been spouting steam on and off over the years, which helped to pick it out of the range.

He hated when he couldn't think of something, but was very happy when he could remember it. If he was close to the volcano, then he was close to Lake Clark. The lake was at the end of many glaciers and the beginning of many other bodies of water that eventually empty into the ocean in Bristol Bay. This one was of the largest lakes in Alaska, being over fifty miles long and the home to a couple hundred people year-round. It was a destination worth trying for. If he could only recognize something, he was confident that he could find his way to safety.

He could see that the trees he'd been in were coming to an end. All he could see in front of him was gravel and large rocks.

"The mudslides must have swept all the vegetation away and left all these rocks behind," he figured.

From the left side of the valley, Mike suddenly heard bushes rustling a short distance away. He stopped to listen. His heart was pounding with anticipation of what it could be. He raised the trash can lid and spear in the direction of the noise, while keeping his revolver and the precious last few bullets holstered. It seemed to get louder and then stop, like something was hunting him. He backed up against some fallen trees so that whatever it was would have to face him. It continued to come at him slowly.

It could be a bear, wolverine or those wolves he knew were following him. The animal was getting close and Mike was ready. His heart was pounding as his adrenaline started to overwhelm him. The small patch of alders close by were the source of this new fear. Mike raised the spear as the noise got close. He thrust his spear at what he thought was a black bear but, stopped just short of putting the knife into the animal when he saw it was just a porcupine.

"AAHHH! You scared the crap out of me!"

The animal puffed itself up to look bigger for protection against predators, obviously scared itself, and began to waddle away as quickly as it could. Mike considered killing it for food, but wasn't sure if it would be very good. He made the decision to let it go, and let out a sigh. He found a place to stop and rest for a moment to regain his senses.

Later that day, while making his way through the last of the fallen trees, he slipped while walking on a log. He tried to catch himself, but his left leg caught between two logs as he fell to his side. He screamed in pain as his weight twisted his leg to the side. He picked himself up as quickly as he could and pulled his foot out from between the logs. He sat there for a while in pain and finally pulled his pant leg up and boot down to assess the injury. It hurt like hell, but he had to look at it and see if it was broken. He didn't want to look at it. If bone were sticking through his skin, he would possibly have infection later to contend with, as well.

He got his pant leg up and could see that he had been lucky. The bone wasn't broken but possibly had a hairline fracture, as he was in quite a bit of pain. A splint would be a good idea before trying to walk on it. If he was lucky, it would heal quickly.

Mike lay back against a tree for a few minutes, breathing through the unbearable pain before trying to move his leg. By the time he was ready to try and move, it was almost dark out. He took his blankets out of the little roll he made with his rope and took his knife off the aluminum pole. He cut one of the blankets into small strips, found a few branches next to him to put all around his leg and make a splint. With the swelling he couldn't put his boot back on, so he sliced the side of the side of it far enough to get his foot in it, then put on the makeshift splint.

Mike drank some water from his canteen, wrapped the remaining blankets around him, lit up a cigarette and tried to relax. The nicotine seemed to help a little, but not nearly enough. Thoughts of home were again flooding through him as tears welled up in his eyes.

"Man up, you son of a bitch," he said to himself. "You will survive and get back home."

He knew he needed to get some sleep. He didn't want to stay exposed out in the open, but was in too much pain to climb a tree or walk anywhere.

His night was dictated by throbbing pain, and sleep rarely came. He needed to get some rest, but every time he drifted off he woke up in agony soon after.

The morning came all too quickly. Mike needed to find a crutch or cane in order to keep going. He wanted to keep his weight off his leg and knew he needed to find help sooner than later. He searched for a suitable stick as he pulled his weight backward, while trying to keep his bad leg straight.

As soon as one was located, the whittling began. Knowing this would dull the knife further, Mike did as little as possible to shape it to work for him. It would be slow going now. After gathering the rest of his belongings, he sat down on a moss covered rock to eat some of the last bit of caribou meat before he started for the day.

The rocks were hard to walk through in his condition, but the makeshift cane and spear made things a little easier.

"Tundra would be much easier until my leg healed," he said. "At least the weather's still pretty good."

No rain made things a little more bearable. The stream continued to wind through the valley, but he maneuvered to pick his way to a section where the rocks were smaller and easier to hobble through. It was very slow going now, but he pressed on.

Night would soon be upon him again, so he started looking for a place to sleep. He found a group of large rocks and figured it would be a good area in which to stay. Mike gathered as many sticks and branches as he could carry over to the rocks, pulled the matches out of a waterproof pocket of his jacket and made a fire.

His leg pulsated with pain and was swollen even more now, so he lay down and elevated it. It started to feel better but he needed ice to bring the swelling down. He took his splint and boot off and crawled down to the stream.

He would submerge it for as long as he could tolerate, then go back to the fire. He put his lower leg into the stream and it wasn't long before it was starting to hurt from the cold, too. He decided he had had enough and went back over to the rocks and his fire to warm up.

Mike painfully put his boot back on and then the makeshift splint. He wasn't in so much pain with his leg being numb from the cold water, but it would be nice to have some painkillers. He put more wood on the fire and tried to get some sleep.

Mike woke up the next morning and was cold. The fire was down to a few embers, so he put more wood on it to warm up before starting for the day.

The valley continued to get smaller and narrower on both sides.

The stream seemed to disappear into the rocks in front of him. There were boulders impeding the way but he found an animal path toward the west that made it easier to bypass. It was either this or turn back. It took quite a while to get through the area. On the other side, the valley opened back up and the stream started to get bigger. There weren't many trees anymore, so the cover for predators was limited, which was in his favor.

Mike looked for a place to stop for the night. After navigating the rocks, his leg was hurting pretty bad. He gathered as much wood as he could find and started a fire. There were only four matches left at this point and fire was going to be a necessity for a while. He still didn't know where he was and the coast could be weeks away, if he was even going in the right direction.

Mike curled up in his deteriorating blanket and his mind drifted to home. It was almost summertime and Rachel should be getting the yard and plants ready, or at least the person she hired would. The boys should be well into peewee baseball season and he was missing it. He missed them all so much. He couldn't die out here in the wilderness. No one would ever find his body or would know what happened to him. How long would his family have to wait before the insurance company would pay them the life insurance? Would the boys have to grow up without a dad or would Rachel meet someone new? Would he be good to Rachel and the boys? He wanted to stop thinking about it and keep his spirits up.

"Just focus on the good times," he told himself.

This would be a nice vacation away from the store and life in the suburbs if he wasn't starving and hurting so bad. Between the complaining customers and nasty co-workers, this was almost better. Mike chuckled a little to himself as he sat in front of the fire enjoying his last partial cigarette.

The night was clear and cold. The moon wasn't visible in the valley, but it brightened up the sky. The stars were bright also. Mike put more wood on the fire and just stared at them as he fell asleep.

He woke up to growling. The fire was almost out. The coals were still glowing red hot, but he couldn't see what it was. He slowly pulled his revolver out of its holster with his right hand and raised the spear with his left. A wolf lunged at him over the embers and was stopped just short of his feet by the spear.

He saw more glowing eyes and fired a round at them as the impaled wolf pulled on the spear as it was dying. With the bright flash of the revolver he estimated at least four more wolves in front of him. Two more rounds were fired before he realized he should stop. He didn't want to deplete his ammo unless he knew for sure he could hit one of them.

The spear was buried in the wolf, but Mike was able to pull it out. He realized how lucky he'd been that the wolf lunged right where the spear was pointed. He built the fire up with the remaining wood and sticks at his side which brightened the area around him. The wolves were still out there, and he didn't know how long it would be until first light.

*If this is the same pack, they're relentless,* he thought.

The light of the fire didn't allow him to see much beyond a few feet in front of him. The wolf at his feet would act as a small barrier against another attack if it happened. Mike was down to four rounds and only three in the revolver. He was hungry, scared and alone. Being lost all by himself for so long was really getting to him. The night dragged on, but light was finally on the horizon.

The other three rounds he had fired at the wolves must not have killed any of the others because there weren't any more lying in front of him or in the area, but there was a faint blood trail. The fire was almost completely out, and Mike could see the whole area in front of him as it got lighter. He drank some water and replaced the empty rounds in his revolver with his last live bullet. He looked at the wolf in front of him and decided to skin it for its fur. His last blanket had seen better days, and this would help keep him warm on his journey. He knew there could be lice on the pelt, but they would eventually die in the cold. This took part of his morning to do it. After skinning the animal he fleshed it with his knife before burning the inside with fire from a stick. This would hopefully stop it from rotting as much and attracting predators. This wasn't the same as tanning, but would have to do for now.

The farther he went up in elevation, the colder it had been getting, so the pelt should help. Mike took some meat off the animal, too. He figured it would taste horrible, but it would sustain him. If he couldn't find any other food he would eat it. After cooking some of the wolf meat he started walking for the day.

Mike finally made it to the top of the mountain as it was getting dark. He couldn't believe what he saw in front of him. How could he make it through this? He was glad he had the wolf pelt and the meat now. He would need both to overcome this next obstacle.

c

# Chapter Twelve: The Glacier

Now he understood why the last few days had been so cold. Mike had been following the water, which now stretched out in front of him as an ice field and a new challenge. The massive sheet of ice laid out in front of him was breathtaking, and alarming at the same time. The jagged chunks sticking up that he would have to negotiate put a feeling of helplessness. It would be dangerous walking on the glacier, especially without the right gear and a hurt leg, but he felt that it was his only option. Growing up playing football and other sports helped. The constant reminder from the coaches to work harder and keep going was ringing in his ears. His competitive nature and being in top physical form were keys to his survival.

Mike decided to walk back a few hundred yards for the night and build a fire by the large crack in the rock wall he had seen before the glacier came into view. He would get some sleep and get an early start the next morning. The walk over the ice could take him hours or even days, not knowing how hard it would be or how far he would have to go. Some glaciers are small and some can be many miles long.

As he sat near the fire looking at his remaining three matches, weighing heavily on his conscience, his mind started to wander again. He missed home. He had tried not to dwell on Rachel and the boys, but he wanted to take out his phone, turn it on and look at their pictures. But he knew the battery was almost dead.

Mike gathered more wood from the surrounding area before all light was lost in order to stay as warm as possible. The new pelt he had harvested from the wolf would help immensely.

The next morning when he woke up the fire was already out so he got up and started walking. Mike was so hungry his head was pounding. He choked down some of the wolf meat he had cooked before and it almost came back up, but he squelched the gagging. He needed to get over this ice field and back to vegetation that would have food for him to catch.

The walk uphill, and with all the cracks in the ice, hurt his leg even more. Parts were slick and he did his best to walk slow, keep his weight off of his hurt leg and not fall down. Other parts were deep snow and he wished he had snowshoes on.

"At least my boots are warm," he said as he walked.

He just focused on his goal and continued on. He had only half a canteen of water, but it would have to last until he could find more that he could trust. He had only been drinking from fast- moving and aerated water that had flowed over rocks. He figured that the rocks cleaned the water every few feet. He used a torn-off part of his t-shirt as a screen before it went into his canteen, too. Boiling it before drinking it would be ideal, but he didn't have the means to do so.

The days were short, but getting longer. Lacking daylight still didn't allow for much time to walk along the frozen ground, but he knew this was his best choice for being rescued, if he was even walking in the right direction.

Mike wanted to build a fire at night to stay warm, but didn't have any wood and was almost out of matches.

At dusk each night, he found a crack or a ledge and cut it into a small ice cave with his knife and the pole, so he had some cover from the wind. Every day felt repetitive except he continued to get weaker.

His second night on the glacier, with the wind blowing and the cold chilling him to the bone, he couldn't get much sleep. He didn't dare walk at night with the dangers of cracks and crevasses in the ice.

Finally dozing off, Mike found himself in the meat locker at the grocery store. It didn't feel like all the other times and he wanted to get out of there, but couldn't find the door. Franticly searching and hearing the cooling fans getting louder, he knew he was in trouble. Trying to stay calm, but getting colder, he finally came across a section of the wall that had some cracks and daylight shining through.

Picking up a meat hook he hit the wall until he had a large- enough hole to crawl through. Once on the other side Mike could see nothing but ice in front of him, and that's when he realized he had been dreaming and had actually crawled out of the hole in which he had been sleeping.

A new day was dawning and it seemed the right time to continue on. The sun shining down on him kept him warmer during the day, which helped his situation.

After the third day on the ice Mike came to a large crevasse and stopped briefly to contemplate his next move.

He knew there was no way he could jump over it with this hurt leg.

The swelling had gone down but he still couldn't put all his weight on it. Even if he was in good health, the boots he had on weren't adequate for ice. It would take longer, but he had to walk to the side of the large break in order to cross it at a smaller point.

The walk uphill on the ice with his cane and spear digging into the snow was taking its toll, so Mike stopped early in the day to rest. He wanted to go on, but couldn't. He found a suitable place to get out of the wind and he curled up to try to get some sleep.

With the wind and the cold Mike couldn't sleep much at all. As soon as it got light he kept going, and this kept him warmer. Having the wolf pelt really helped.

"If it wasn't for you, I would have frozen by now, or gotten hypothermia," he murmured as he petted the fur he had been wearing from head to toe like a cape.

The wolf had been so large that he was able to cover most of his own body with the pelt.

He had to get off of the ice and get something to eat. The wind was picking up again and the snow blowing off the ground was making it hard to see.

The solar radiation bouncing off the ice combined with the wind made Mike wish he had sunglasses. He was able to cover most of his exposed skin but some parts would pay the price. His neck was hurting and he hoped it was just from wind burn, not frostbite. He had been able to cover most of his face with his undershirt, but some of it hurt as well. Wind or sunburn was a concern, but frostbite was a completely different story.

The glacier forked to the east around the mountain. It was a 50/50 choice, and Mike took the path in which he had already been going. Was it the right choice? He would soon find out.

"I've been going east, south and southeast, so why change now?" he mumbled to himself.

This way went downhill almost right away, so Mike moved to the right side where the larger rocks were. He would climb down the rocks if he had to so he didn't slip and slide down the hard, wind-blown surface.

There were small trees starting to show up in all directions the farther he walked down the mountain, and it was warmer now.

There was fog cover below, so what lay in front of him was hidden. Mike ate some tree buds to try to sustain him until he could find something more substantive. The walk down the rocks was a completely different hurt on his leg.

As soon as he found a couple of rocks that could hide him for the night, Mike settled in. It was warmer on this side of the mountain, and with the cover from the rocks he would hopefully be able to get more sleep.

His gloves were falling apart and he hoped he didn't have to negotiate any more ice. He thought about just leaving them behind, but what if he needed something on his hands again? They would stay in the pockets of his parka for now.

That night, the clouds cleared and the northern lights could be seen. He had seen pictures of the Aurora Borealis before, but had never thought he would have experienced them unless he was farther north. They started out just a glimmer and got brighter, mostly, bright green, with white and then red mixed in. The colors blended together to form shades of pink and almost purple. They seemed to dance in the sky.

"Wow," he caught himself saying out loud at the peak of the show.

The light show lasted for hours before finally dissipating from view. He knew he had just experienced nature in the raw, and had no one with which to share it.

The next morning Mike started to negotiate the large rocks and soon heard rushing water. An eagle was circling above, between him and the low-lying clouds. The majestic bird continually looked down and was losing elevation. Mike looked around and finally saw what it was looking at. A hare was making its way down through the rocks in front of him. With his injuries, Mike knew the eagle had more of a chance at getting it than he did, so he didn't even try.

There was still fog in front of him, but he pressed on slowly. What came into view took his breath away.

# Chapter Thirteen: Paradise

As Mike climbed down next to a waterfall at the end of the glacier he saw a lush green valley open up in front of him. He knew at this moment that he had made the correct choice the day before. If he had taken the other fork on the glacier, would he still be on it, out in the cold? The green bushes and trees were a welcome sight after the days he had spent on the ice with no food. The first priority was looking for something to eat. Mike filled his canteen in the water flowing from the waterfall. When he brought the canteen up to his lips, he felt instant pain and realized they were blistered. With the cold and dehydration they had gotten this way pretty fast. He carefully drank as much as he could and made his way down to the bottom of the valley where a river was waiting for him.

"The head waters must be up at the other end of the glacier," he figured.

He stopped for a minute and realized that he hadn't had a cigarette in about a week. He wasn't craving one and had been so busy staying alive that the withdrawals never even registered. He didn't need the habit anyway. It made his breath and clothes stink and, Rachael never liked it either. He would be healthier, too. Though, if he hadn't found the pack in the plane he might not have been able to make it through the ordeal this far. He had used them as a mental crutch, and they had worked.

With the ice behind him and trees in front of him, he thought, there should be birds or small animals to hunt. With only four rounds left in his revolver he had to choose his shots more carefully than ever.

The valley continued to open up in front of him as the day dragged on and even though he was hurting, the possibilities that lay before him kept him going.

There was finally wood for a fire, so Mike found a spot that looked good for the night. As he was gathering wood he noticed a small bull moose crossing the river. Overcome with excitement he slowly set the wood down and watched the animal. It was dark in color and had small nubs protruding from between its ears. He wanted to shoot it but knew most of the meat would go bad before he could eat it all. He was very hungry and knew that he was getting too skinny. The moose was coming in his direction as if it hadn't even seen him, and it might not have, due to swimming in the river. Mike pulled his revolver from his chest holster and pointed it at the animal as it got closer.

"Steady," Mike said to himself softly as the revolver swayed back and forth.

As soon as the creature made it completely out of the water, Mike shot. The small bull fell right over. It was a good shot right in the head from about thirty feet away.

"Just like all the other times, now the work begins," he said.

Mike bled the moose, started skinning from its back quarters and worked his way to the head. There was no need to gut the animal when he was just taking the legs. It wasn't very warm outside, but he had to cool it off so it didn't spoil. Steam was rising from it as he peeled back the layers. The warmth of the animal felt nice on his hands as he continued the task.

"Hard winter for you, wasn't it, buddy?" Mike said to his kill as he noticed there wasn't much fat on it.

He knew that quite a bit of it would go bad, but there was nothing he could do about that. Carving around the shoulders and hip joints, he slowly removed each quarter from the body and placed them on the carcass so they wouldn't get dirty.

He was now down to just three rounds in his revolver, and with this kill there would be more predators with which to contend.

After skinning the game he then took a break to find a suitable place to hole up for a while that would be more defensible than what he had already found.

Slowly getting up after sitting on the rocks wasn't easy. Mike moved over to the river to wash his hands and knife and then started looking at the rocky hillside of the river valley. There were many areas with water trickling or flowing down the mountain. He needed a dry spot, preferably something with a cliff above to keep the rain off if the weather turned bad.

A few hundred yards down the river he found the perfect place. There were alders above and some spruce trees all set back in some rocks. He had great cover and would be able to see for a long distance in three directions. The moose was still cooling off, so he went up to the spot he had found and started clearing an area to make it livable for as long as he needed. There was no point in leaving all the meat if he could eat for a week or more before it went bad.

After getting the area ready, Mike went back to the kill to start bringing quarters to the camp. Once he reached the moose, he decided to take some rib bones and fashion them as weapons. He could do this with some of the leg bones, too, once they dried out.

His leg was feeling better being on dry, flat ground, but he was ready to get off of it completely and let it heal.

The smell of the blood would start to attract hungry animals within days, if they didn't smell it already.

He didn't have enough rope to hang all the quarters, so he only took three of them along with the back strap and the heart. He would hang two and cook one after the tender parts were gone.

With all the rocks in the immediate area Mike decided to try something he had seen on one of those survival shows. He made a deep fire pit and put a large, flat rock over the top to use as a grill. He had done something similar with the caribou, but this would be better.

After getting the fire burning hot, he put some water on the flat rock to clean it off and steam rose from it right away. A few strips of meat he had cut were placed on the rock and they started to cook within a few minutes.

"I have my own barbecue pit," Mike said.

He had to watch the meat and was salivating while continually turning it, or it would stick to the rock. Moose meat was very lean compared to beef, and didn't have the fat content needed to not stick.

By the time everything was done cooking it was almost dark and Mike was exhausted, but was ready to devour his prey. He took the first bite of real food he had had in days.

"Damn, you're a good cook," he said, congratulating himself. "Even without seasoning, this is fantastic!"

Slowly chewing and enjoying each bite, Mike felt comfort in knowing that, despite the predicament he was in, he was still alive.

He had food and shelter for now, so he was happy. He fell asleep by a warm fire with a belly full of meat. The rest of the fortification would be done the next day.

He woke the next day to a squawk. Ignoring the bird this time, he noticed the sun was out and shining bright through the branches above. Birds were chirping and it sounded like a church choir singing.

The fire had burned down to coals, so he added more wood to rejuvenate it. It had to burn constantly due to the lack of matches.

He figured he had slept well past early morning and knew it had been desperately needed. Mike looked carefully at his surroundings and at the meat. He would have to fortify the area better, but having the advantage of being uphill made him feel better already.

He could see the moose carcass from his spot on the mountain and it was still in the same place he had left it, and he was glad for that. His leg felt better, but he decided to continue to use the crutch and spear to keep as much weight off of it as possible. He went down to the river and washed up. The cold water on his face was refreshing and woke him up. He started his day by making the small fire bigger to cook some more meat, this time with tree buds for flavor, and then he gathered more wood before resting again. Mike knew that this was his chance to heal and regain his strength.

"It's not like I have anywhere else to go right now," he mumbled.

With the meat hanging in the trees, it would stay very cool during the day with the natural shade from the branches. With no meat sacks to cover the quarters, they would be an easy target for bees and flies.

Mike had an idea about how to make the meat last longer and keep insects away. If he could gather large chunks of ice from farther up on the mountain and pack it all around the meat, it would act as a refrigerator and maybe a freezer. If he cooked it first and then put it in the ice, it should last even longer.

Mike's idea of bringing the ice to his makeshift camp was taking a toll on his leg that hadn't yet healed properly. He needed some of the ice to bring the swelling down after a long day up and down the mountain.

He planned to stay at his camp for a couple of days to rest and keep all his weight off his leg. The morning of the second day he woke early to the sound of growling. It was dawn and hard to see, as only a glimmer of light was on the horizon. Mike clung to his spear and gripped his revolver. The sound he heard was too close for comfort. He made his way to a tree that overlooked the river and could see some animals silhouetted near the moose carcass. He had to wait until more light allowed him to see what was causing the commotion. A brown bear sow and three cubs were feasting on the moose, and there was a black bear closing in on them.

"This should be interesting," he commented under his breath.

The black bear approached the kill and the very large sow charged it. She was protecting her cubs and the meal at the same time. The sow ran straight into the black bear and the two of them rolled into the river.

The sound of the fight was intimidating as the *roars* and *growls* emitted from the animals echoed down the valley. Mike had never seen anything like it, not even on TV.

The black bear made its way out of the water with the sow right behind it. They rolled on the rocks and the sow gained the advantage. Tearing the black bear open with her large claws. Mike figured the black bear must have been an adolescent and didn't have much fighting experience. That and the mama bear was pissed.

Throughout the fight, the cubs just ate on the moose, looking over from time to time to keep an eye on mom. Mike thought this was funny and was smiling for the first time in weeks. This spectacle had been incredible, a secret nature show all for him. Despite losing some meat, the show was worth it. The next best thing would be getting rescued and going home. The bears ate their fill and eventually moved on later that day, after napping by the carcass.

His leg was starting to feel better, but he knew that it was far from healed. The ice he had gotten for the meat and his leg was almost gone. He was hoping to continue to control the swelling still, so he went to get more.

One of the quarters he had brought up was being eaten by various bugs as it hung in the trees, he discovered one day. Mike pulled it down, and it smelled sour and rotten. He quickly separated it from the rest of the meat and hoped that the remaining quarter wouldn't have this problem. He took the ruined quarter over to the moose carcass so the rotten meat was all in one place. Ravens and other birds had been picking at it after the bears had their fill, and it was slowly disappearing.

The week at the camp above the river went by quickly and, surprisingly, so did the rest of the meat from the moose. Mike had been eating it all day, in an effort to build up his strength. The fire that he started when he set up camp had kept burning the entire time he was there. There was always warmth and protection from predators. The fire was positioned right in front of the area he had made into a small fortress. Old logs and rocks were positioned on the sides and his back was at the mountain. Spruce branches were piled up on the ground with the wolf pelt on top of those, which made the best bed he could hope for.

It had rained a little while he was there and the rock shelter tucked in the trees really helped keep him dry, and was better than sleeping in a tree. The sound of the river flowing down below helped him sleep at night. This wasn't as nice as the cabin in which he had stayed, but it worked for the time he occupied it. The journey had to continue now, with most of the meat gone. He would leave in the morning.

# Chapter Fourteen: The Dam

The river continued to get bigger as he plodded along the next day, but now night was beginning to fall. Sleeping in a tree again was not going to be the most welcome place compared to the palace he had of his last camp, but was necessary. Mike found a nice tree and climbed it for the night.

The next morning before climbing down he decided to look around and search the area. Mike couldn't believe what he saw in front of him in the river. He climbed up the side of the mountain and sat on some large rocks for a better view after getting out of the tree.

There was a beaver dam stretching across the valley, bigger than any he had seen before. Large trees were mixed in with spruce and alders branches, while two large mounds could be seen by the edges.

"They must have a whole family working on this thing," he said.

Mike had been wondering why the river had slowed down and got bigger as he walked along it. Being retained by the dam, was a very big lake. He had been traveling on the west side of the river after walking off the glacier, but couldn't continue due to the wetlands and steep cliffs on that side past the dam. His only other choice was crossing the beaver's home.

The other side looked like it was pretty flat for many miles before he couldn't see what remained of the river anymore as it went around a bend.

There were many large trees floating that would help him cross, but if he slipped and fell in between them with the current pushing against them, he was done for.

Climbing down from his perch Mike located what he thought was the best place to start crossing. With extreme caution he started picking his way, crawling over the dam.

The first section that he crossed wasn't bad. Once he got to the middle and the water got deeper all of the logs and branches were just floating. The current was the strongest here, too, but the branches were secured together thanks to the engineering of the beavers. Mike had to crawl and stay on the largest of the logs. He was getting wet all over as the dam sank with his weight, and he was starting to shiver.

The makeshift spear and trashcan lid were tied to his back with the chunk of rope. He took care not to lose them as he crept along, feeling for them regularly verifying they were still there.

Some of the branches and logs started to float over the edge of the dam into the river. He knew he had to hurry or it could all give way and he would either be swimming or floating on logs. With much relief he reached the opposite side just as a large portion of the dam floated away. Water gushed through, rushing downstream.

"There's going to be one upset beaver once he sees what I did," he mumbled.

Safely on the other side he set about building a fire to warm up. He saw a couple of large trees and limped toward them.

"Only two matches left, damn", he cursed.

He carefully covered some small sticks and last year's dry brown leaves to make sure they caught fire. Later, when he was warm and dry out, he could climb one of the trees for the night.

Mike gathered sticks and larger chunks of wood as fast as he could while the small sticks and leaves continued to burn brighter. The flames slowly grew and he was able to build them up larger with more wood. This helped warm him up a little, but he was still shaking uncontrollably. The water was coming from the melting glacier and was extremely cold.

The fire was soon going better and he was starting to warm up. He took his outer layer of clothes off and propped them up on sticks so they could dry quicker. This whole process hurt his leg and he was glad he wouldn't be going anywhere for the night.

The sun was going down now and he hadn't made it very far that day. After warming up and drying out, Mike looked at the lake and wondered why he hadn't at least brought some fishing line and gear with him from the cabin, let alone a pole.

"What were you thinking?" he chastised himself.

He knew why. It wasn't his stuff so he put it all back where he had found it. He didn't think about coming upon another lake, either. There was still a little bit of moose meat left in his pocket, and he could hunt for birds, too.

Just before it got too dark to see, the fire was dimming, and exhaustion was taking hold. He headed to a tree for the night, with the sound of the water willing him to sleep. If it had been too quiet, he would have thought something was wrong and couldn't have slept. He was still cold from getting wet, even though he was dry now and his shivering stalled off sleep.

The morning came after a fitful night. He had gotten used to sleeping in the bed he had made on the ground.

"A bed is going to feel strange if I make it home. No, when I make it home," he said with confidence as he climbed down the tree.

The coals from the fire were still smoking, so he decided to re-build the fire and heat some meat for breakfast. He got it going again after blowing on the ashes with some dry needles and small sticks on top. He added kindling to get it bigger and went to the lake to splash some water on his face.

The lake looked calm and peaceful as he got to the edge. Reflections of the trees and mountains could be seen in parts of it. A loon could be heard calling somewhere on the other side. The bugle echoed across as the morning fog hanging on the water slowly burned off when the sun's rays pierced through with rainbow-like colors.

The dam was almost completely repaired. He figured the beavers had been up all night once they found the damage.

"At least the weather's good," Mike commented, looking up at the sky.

As he was walking back to the fire Mike saw a grouse on the ground in some bushes. He knew they would be laying eggs soon, so he moved in with his spear.

"I can get meat and eggs," he said under his breath.

Sure enough another grouse, partially white but turning brown, was swooping in to try to get him out of the area, probably its mate due to the red above its eyes. Squawking and flying low in front of him, the bird was relentless. The one on the ground wasn't moving even as he closed in. He thrust his spear into the bushes, just missing the bird as it flew away. There were four small eggs underneath of it, however. The eggs were less than half the size of a chicken's and brown with black spots on them. He wanted to cook them, but had no frying pan. He did have the trash can lid. The galvanized and rusted lid would have to be used to boil water and then the eggs. He could then take the eggs with him to be eaten later.

"Just when things on this trip start to get dull, they turn right back around," said Mike. "I wonder if I'm talking to myself too much. Nah, I'm not going crazy yet."

He built the fire up with rocks around it, this time to hold the trash can lid so it didn't fall over with the water in it.

The eggs took longer to cook than he had hoped. The water didn't boil for some time, but it wasn't like he had any place to be. After cooking the eggs, he warmed some already cooked moose meat he pulled out of his pocket.

Late that morning Mike had hard boiled eggs and cooked meat. The taste of the eggs was a nice treat from all the meat on which he'd been feasting.

Once he was done eating he put the fire out and packed his meager belongings. The long stretch of sand and rocks turned into tundra and then trees. The lake on the other side of the river was being fed by another glacier on the adjacent mountains. It was very long and widened as the valley opened up.

The next two days passed without any problems. His leg was hurting again as he continued, but he had to push himself if he was going to find help.

From time to time Mike felt like he was being watched. Chills went down his spine each time he would hear squirrel's chatter or a marmot whistle. It meant that something was too close to them, or maybe they were yelling at him. The feeling went on for days and he didn't like it at all.

# Chapter Fifteen:
# Final Stand

On the second morning, after leaving his sanctuary by the river, Mike was walking along the lake with cooperative weather and not much happening. Out of the tree-line walked a massive brown bear boar. The gigantic animal noticed him almost instantly and moved to intercept. Without hesitation Mike pulled his revolver and backed up against a tree as the monster came at him. He put the spear against it and pointed it straight ahead as the bear charged in. He got one round off and thrust the spear into the beast before being pushed down to the ground. The revolver was knocked out of his hand as he was slammed hard onto the moss-covered rocks. Mike curled up and covered his head as the bear swatted him around like a ping-pong ball.

Out of nowhere there was growling, then a wolf was biting the bear, and then two more wolves were on it. The bruin was swatting the big canines around, but they just kept going back at it. The bear had been shot and stabbed but was still winning the fight against three wolves.

One wolf was limping away and the other two were badly hurt. Mike was dazed but looked around and found his revolver. After fumbling to get it back into his hand he took aim and yelled as loud as he could. The bear turned and stood up, towering above him just a few feet away as the wolves were regrouping. He shot the bear in the chest and it fell down. The wolves were instantly on it again, tearing away at its throat as the third one came back to join in. There was blood everywhere as the wolves made certain the bear was dead.

Mike slumped against the nearest tree, expecting death to join him. The wolves stopped and looked at him. Blood dripped from their mouths as they growled. He could see their big white teeth as he sat broken and bloody on the ground. The wolves finished ripping the bear's throat and looked up at him again. They locked eyes briefly before Mike looked away. He could hear the largest wolf walking closer and closer to him. Too scared to look up, the sound of footsteps continued to move nearer.

He reflected on his life and all the time he had wasted leading up to this point. He thought about how fucking pointless his life had been and how perhaps it would be better for his family if he just died here and now. They would get life insurance money from his death and be happier without him in the picture.

"This is it," he said.

He felt tears forming in his eyes, stinging his eyelids as his body forced the remainder of whatever water he had left in him to form one last tear.

He couldn't hear the footsteps anymore, and with his eyes closed, he wouldn't see the end coming.

Moments passed, and he could feel the hot breath of the wolf on his face. He looked up as if regaining his strength and met eyes with the massive creature. He could sense the animal's pain and confusion. He blinked and felt the wet tear, the remainder of his life, run down the lines of his face. The wolf caught the tear with its tongue before it fell to the ground. She continued to lick his face, warming him with every aggressive lick. She stopped and looked at the other two momentarily, as if hearing their thoughts, before moving away from him.

Mike sat there in amazement, not understanding what had just happened, as the animals quietly slipped away through the brush.

"Was it the wolf pelt?" he wanted to ask them as they disappeared.

His wet face was covered in wolf saliva, his blood and bear blood. He was hurt badly and needed to tend to his wounds. He got up, using every last bit of strength left in him, holstered his revolver and located the broken spear with his knife on it. He just wanted to get as far away from the area as possible.

A few hundred yards away he stopped and sat down on a rock. His left arm was cut open and bleeding. Most of the lower part of the sleeve of the parka was missing. His injured leg was throbbing. He hadn't realized how hurt he was until the adrenalin had stopped rushing through his veins.

Mike put pressure on the cut but it wouldn't stop bleeding. He wrapped a piece of his t-shirt around his bicep to slow the flow and gathered wood for a fire. He had to cauterize the wound or risk bleeding to death.

He was down to his last match to start the fire. Carefully striking the match and moving it down to the leaves and small sticks was hard, as he was shaking so much, but as the flames came to life he knew he had been successful.

After the fire was roaring, Mike put the skinning knife into the coals to heat it up and sterilize it. His arm was going numb, so he relieved the pressure. Blood squirted out of the wound and he cinched the t-shirt back down.

He pulled the knife out of the fire and it, was glowing red hot. He wiped the blood away so he could see the cut better and started sealing it from the edges. It would be a large scar once it healed, but it had to be done. Mike was screaming in pain each time he touched the blade to his arm.

Once he was satisfied it was completely cauterized, he released the pressure slowly. His arm hurt badly. He poured water from his canteen on the wound and then drank the rest.

He then moved on to his leg. It was throbbing with every beat of his heart. He was in agony with the wounds he had sustained in the mauling. He still couldn't figure out why the wolves helped him and then left him alone. He was grateful for the assistance, yet baffled at the same time.

# Chapter Sixteen:
# Desperation

Out of water and injured, Mike had to find shelter.
He took to a tree early that night and didn't climb very
far up it. He was down to one bullet in his revolver, no
more matches and the spear was broken. The handle on
the trash can lid had broken off, too, and was basically
useless now, so he would be leaving it behind. The pain
from his injuries kept him up throughout the night. As
soon as there was light on the horizon, Mike made his
way down the tree and warmed up on the coals of the
fire he had made the day before. The first priority was
finding water and then suitable shelter on the ground.
He couldn't keep climbing trees in his condition. The
water was the easy part with all the snow melting from
the mountains above. He found a stream quickly. The
walk was agonizing that morning on the reinjured leg.
He stuck to the lake, praying to see a hunting cabin or
a tent with hunters, campers or hikers.

Mike meandered around a bend in the lake and
saw another beach. The closer he got he could see a
small cabin just on the other side of a stream.

"Can I be this lucky?" he said, wondering if it was
a mirage.

After taking a break and reassuring himself that
it was real, he found a tree that had fallen across the
stream and crossed there.

Hobbling up to the cabin, it looked as if it was a landmark because of a flagpole and sign he could see as he approached it. The pain was so bad that he didn't look at them, just went inside after getting the door open. There was a bed, table, chairs, fireplace and wood stove inside, most of the comforts of home. He closed the door and collapsed on the bed.

When he woke up, he had no idea how long he had slept. There was light peeking through a few cracks, so he figured he had slept through the night and part of the next day. He walked over to the door and opened it. It was raining out, but clearly daytime.

The lake was just a short distance away and the stream for fresh water was close, too. Mike took off his parka and proceeded to go down to the lake and wash up.

After the well-needed sleep, he felt better, yet still in pain. He went over to the stream and filled his canteen, drinking his fill, refilling it, and then walking back.

Once he got the shutter parts covering the windows of the cabin open, the next task would be to find food firewood and a stash of matches.

The sign on the outside of the cabin was not all visible as he walked up to it. He could make out Lake Clark National Park and Re...Twin Lakes and Ric... The sign was either very old or damaged from the winter. Regardless, at least he had an idea of where he was. The national park was massive, but at least he knew it was a place others visited.

The weather looked as if it might get worse so pain and all, he went in search of something to eat. As he walked past the back of the cabin he saw firewood stacked all the way to the roof. An outhouse was out back also with tools hanging from under the eaves. A shovel, saw and axe caught his attention. Mike didn't know whose cabin this was, but it had been there for quite some time and it looked like someone lived there.

*It couldn't be a hunting cabin,* he thought, *being in the valley. A hunter would have to walk for miles from here to find a good area to hunt moose or caribou.*

It didn't matter. For now, Mike had a secure place to rest and heal. Finding food was the priority now that he had everything else he would need.

*Birds would be the easiest to get even being injured,* he thought.

After a few hours of hunting, Mike was hurting and getting soaked from the rain. He had only been able to get a squirrel and made his way back to the cabin.

He cleaned the game in the stream and took it to cut up on the table inside the cabin. He went out back to get wood for the stove and fireplace. Mike discovered a whole box of matches on the mantle above the stove that would last him quite a while.

He hung up all his wet gear to let it dry and was able to relax in a chair for the first time in weeks.

It was warming up in the cabin after building the fire, so he decided to take his boots off and look at his leg and blisters. His arm looked bad once he got to it, but there wasn't much he could do. Keeping it clean was his only medical option for now.

There were some candles and a lantern on the shelf above the woodstove. He lit them so he could look around his new shelter as the light shining through the windows went away.

"This had to have been built by some old home-steader decades ago," he said to himself.

There were a couple of fishing poles in the corner and Mike hoped he had all the gear he needed to catch some fish.

With any luck, someone would fly out and check on the cabin, considering what was in it. The evening meal was a small one, but better than nothing.

Mike's clothes were drying out and he fell asleep once again on the bed. He woke up to thunder and realized that the lantern and candles were still burning. He got up and put them out after putting more wood in the woodstove.

The next day it was still raining with very low clouds when Mike went outside to try and catch some fish. There was little wind, but the low clouds and fog would make it so no planes would be flying.

He found some worms under an old log and hoped they would do the job. The worms were small, so he put two on for starters. With a scant amount of line on the old pole, the fish would have to be close to shore. He had a small bobber, one weight and a rusted hook, so Mike cast the small amount of line out off the pole as far as he could. The bobber hit the water with a splash. Almost instantly he had a fish on. Instead of reeling, he just slowly walked backward until the fish was on shore and flopped off the hook. It wasn't very big, but would be edible all the same. As he approached, it flopped back into the water before he was able to secure it. He repeated his action a couple more times and was finally successful at landing a few.

With his leg and arm hurting so much, he slowly made his way back to the cabin, fish in tow.

The weather continued to deteriorate and he was glad for the shelter and so many more luxuries than the last cabin had offered. He would be able to relax here, regain his strength and heal after yet another ordeal.

The fish fried up nicely in the large frying pan he found hanging on the wall. The small cabin was stocked with many items that would be useful in the coming days, including some seasonings and cooking supplies. Having a warm, dry place was like heaven compared to what he had been through. Salt and pepper was downright orgasmic.

The days in the cabin with the bad weather outside might normally have felt slow, but Mike wasn't feeling well with his injuries and welcomed the rest. His body, feeling, broken and bruised, needed to heal and sleep was the best thing for him, since he lacked medical supplies.

The harsh weather on the lake lasted for three days and looked as if it might let up so he could catch more fish or hunt.

Sleeping for most of each day passed the time faster while the spring storm raged on. When he woke, he only stoked the fire and went back to sleep.

His arm was hurting more and more as time passed. He figured it might be infected, due to the redness and being very hot, but what could he do? Mike kept it as clean as he could with water he heated on the woodstove, but it didn't seem to be getting much better.

"At least you don't have puss coming out of you yet," he said to his wound.

The rain let up and the sun came out, so he ventured outside to try to catch some fish late one afternoon.

After catching a few fish, Mike made his way slowly back up to the cabin.

"At least I have shelter, food and a way to stay warm," he said staring at his new home.

He wondered again if anyone would come and check on the cabin. He felt the need to start walking down the lake soon, but hesitated to leave another shelter and fire.

"I can't be the only one out here. I have to find help," Mike mumbled to himself, yet knowing the area was vast.

The days continued to pass and he was finally starting to feel better. The howling of wolves in the distance some nights reminded him about how the pack had treated him. He was still confused, but was glad it turned out the way it did.

He decided to go hunting and see if he could find something farther down the beach on another part of the lake.

Mike made another cane to help stabilize his walk. Now that his leg was feeling better he would be able to do more. He filled the fireplace and stove with as much wood as they could take and pocketed all the supplies he could carry. If he got lost or decided to continue on, he would need the matches and some of the other supplies he had found in and around the cabin. He brought a fishing pole this time. He had learned many things on his journey of survival and kept telling himself that he would never leave home without a survival pack ever again. He continually made a mental list of what he needed to put in it.

With his arm hurting, the journey would be slow, but he needed to see what was on the rest of the lake. Small streams crossed his path as he walked along.

"Snow-melt from the mountains," Mike deduced as he crossed yet another stream.

After a few hours and seeing nothing but trees, tundra and more beaches, Mike stopped to rest and snack on some fish he had cooked the night before.

A raven flew overhead while he took his break. There was no squawking so he figured it wasn't his stalker bird.

After eating and resting a while, he continued to press on. With hours of seeing nothing of consequence, Mike was resting again, this time by a large spruce tree, when he heard a cooing sound. Looking around, he finally spotted some Spruce Grouse in the tree. They were camouflaged by the color on their feathers. He remembered that Ted and John called them stupid chickens because they would just sit there and let you kill them. He carefully moved the spear into position and thrust it into a bird. The rest flew away a short distance, so he tried his luck again and ended up with two birds, not wanting to waste more energy following the rest of them.

Mike was making his way through the trees when he heard something in front of him. A lynx appeared a short distance away. The large cat stopped for a brief moment and looked at him, then disappeared into the trees.

"He must have been hunting birds too," Mike said to himself.

The path around the lake slowly transitioned to up-hill with cliffs appearing where there had been beaches along the lake. Mike continued so he would know what was in front of him for the inevitable trek that lay ahead. The mountains grew close, which concerned him.

Mike pressed on over the small hill in front of him to see what was on the other side. His leg hurt worse going uphill. The cane helped, but it was slow going as he climbed. He finally reached the top and fell to the ground. It was a steep cliff and no more beach for as far as he could see. He broke down and tears welled up in his eyes. He felt defeated.

"Come on! Really, is this how it's going to be now? This can't be happening," he said, letting out a loud sigh.

He would have to walk back miles and start up the mountainside to bypass these cliffs if he wanted to move on. As he sat there, he saw something off in the distance on the lake below. It looked like a canoe and people rowing it. He stood up and began yelling like a maniac.

"Help! Help me, please," he yelled, over and over.

They were too far away to hear him and the flash of hope of finally going home and seeing his family slowly dissipated as he could see they were moving away from him.

It would be dark soon. He had two choices, walk back to the cabin and start again at first light or start a fire here and hope they saw it. He would be exposed to the elements and predators if he stayed, but it was worth the risk if they saw him. Without a canoe, he couldn't get to them unless he walked up the mountain and traversed it to get over there. Would they still be there if he went to all that trouble? Mike decided to go back to the cabin as the canoe, disappeared behind the trees on the bend of the lake. He would figure out what to do when he got back to the cabin.

The walk back took a little longer as the day had taken its toll on him physically and mentally. Mike had seen the first sign of people in weeks and couldn't even get their attention. It would take him days to get to where he thought they were, and they might be gone by then. In his condition, he had to do something else.

Once Mike saw the smoke coming from the chimneys as he approached, he had a plan.

When he entered the cabin it was warm, but the fires were almost out. The coals were hot so he put more wood on them and it brightened the place back up as they caught fire.

He would build an S.O.S. fire on the beach the following day. The people on the lake had to have been flown out to go camping or fishing, maybe hunting. If a plane flew over-head and saw just a fire on the beach, the pilot might not think much of it. If the fire were in the shape of a giant S.O.S., they would hopefully land and find out if someone needed help.

His plan would take a lot of time and effort to get all the wood in place. He would light it in the early evening and hopefully it would burn most of the night if he could keep putting wood on it.

Mike cleaned and cooked the birds he had gotten that day and ate most of the meat. He needed his rest and strength, but continued to think about what he was going to do tomorrow, and struggled to fall asleep.

The next morning an internal alarm clock went off in Mike's head and he woke and could see light on the horizon. The weather was still good, motivating him to execute his plan. After a brief morning meal of hot grouse broth, Mike grabbed his small rope and went out back to get the shovel hanging up on the rack. He left the rope by the axe and the saw, which he planned to use later if he needed them.

Mike found a spot on the beach that would be visible from just about anywhere. There could be hunters in the nearby mountains, too. The vastness of the area could hold many hikers and hunters, but being so spread out they might never come across each other.

Many trees were lying on the ground, blown over by the wind, no doubt, and these would be dry and seasoned. They would be ideal for burning, much better than green wood. He would use these as a last resort or to restock what he was taking from the pile later. Mike was already exhausted from digging the trenches on the beach and his arm complained badly, but he pushed through the near-crippling discomfort. He got to work cutting the rounds of wood with the axe and dragging the bundles down to the beach using the rope tied to him.

The job wasn't the easiest thing he had ever done, and he knew it would take at least two days at his current pace. The firewood was stacked in each trench to maximize the burning capability and hopefully last longer.

Would the people still be there when he was ready to light it and would the weather hold out? It didn't really matter. He would get done and light the signal fire when it was ready.

After many hours and only being partially done, Mike took a break to eat. He wanted to take a nap, but knew it would only take him that much longer to finish. He was about out of food again and needed to catch more fish if he was going to have enough energy to continue.

The sun was going down and the fish were jumping as he brought another load of wood down to the beach. He was a little over half done with the project and knew he needed to get some food. He stopped for the night and went to get a fishing pole. Mike only caught a few fish before he decided to quit.

"I know I won't have any problems sleeping tonight," he said to himself as he cleaned the fish at the edge of the lake.

The knife had been brand new when he left on the hunting trip, but was beginning to dull with so much use. He hoped it would stay sharp enough for what he needed it for.

Walking back to the cabin was harder this time and Mike knew he would be very sore the next morning. He had to continue. When he was rescued, it would all be worth his efforts.

The fish cooked up nicely and after stoking the fireplace for the night, he instantly fell asleep.

The next morning it was lighter out and he knew he had slept longer than he wanted to.

"Why didn't you set the alarm?" he questioned himself as he looked at his watch, seeing it was almost 10 a.m.

Mike sat up in bed and could barely move his arm. He took his shirt off and it didn't look good. If it wasn't infected before, it was now. The scabs were oozing puss and he felt feverish. He had taken care of it the best he could with what he had, but knew it wouldn't be long before he was in real trouble. He had to finish the signal fire.

He ate some of the fish from the night before, grabbed his canteen and cane and went outside to start his task. He stopped by the outhouse on his way to the firewood area. His diet had made it so anything he ate went right through him and this was just causing more issues and discomfort, though the outhouse with toilet paper was luxury at this point.

Being as sore as he was, the day dragged on, but he finally got all the wood in place. Once he started the fires they should burn for many hours before he needed to put more wood on them. He planned on staying outside for most of the night and putting more wood on them before retiring to the cabin.

It was late afternoon when he got all of them lit, and after awhile was getting hungry. He saw some ducks flying above the cabin, so he decided to try to catch them. Mike moved past the cabin and followed them down the lake with spear in hand.

# Chapter Seventeen:
# Lost and Confused

Mike suddenly found himself in the meat locker at the grocery store. The sides of beef were slowly swinging back and forth.

"Did we just have an earthquake?" he mumbled.

He was confused, but the cold air and the sound of the fans made him feel at ease. The fans slowly turned off and he was standing in silence. The flanks of beef were no longer moving. Mike left the locker and moved out into the store. There were people everywhere, but they acted like he wasn't there. He tried greeting a few people, but got no response back from them.

"Why is this happening and why are you ignoring me?" he asked them.

Mike continued to walk through the store. His cell-phone was ringing, but where was it? He reached in his pocket, but he couldn't locate it. He made his way to the end of the next aisle, and then there was nobody in the store. The ringing was getting closer, but where was the phone? As Mike got to the bakery he could see the lights at that end of the store were flickering and the kitchen was completely dark. He found his phone over by the donuts.

"How did it get over here?" he wondered.

Caller ID said Rachael, so he answered it.

"Hello Rachael," he said.

There was only a muffled voice on the other end. He tried moving to an area where he could get better reception, but it continued to be muffled until the call failed.

He heard a noise and walked into the bakery. It was pitch black and he needed a moment to let his eyes adjust. Mike suddenly felt as if he was stepping off a cliff and began falling.

He woke up confused, cold and on the ground at the base of a tree, completely disorientated. It was bright daylight out and he figured it must be the next day. The last thing he remembered was going after the ducks he had seen by the cabin after lighting the signal fire.

He stood up groggily. The cane he had made was nowhere to be found and his arm hurt badly. He figured he must have somehow walked to this area, but why, and where were his things? He didn't recognize his surroundings and fear enveloped him. He tried to get his bearings, but everything was blurry and he was having a hard time seeing very far. He was franticly looking around and checking to see what he had on his person. He still had his revolver on his chest, and decided to look through his pockets to do an inventory. He had his knife, the small box of matches, and that was it. No canteen, no crutches or fishing pole.

"Not good," he commented. "What the hell is going on?"

Despair, anger and helplessness were overtaking him as he tried to remember what had happened.

"I lit the fire and then I left. Did anyone show up? Are they looking for me now? Damn you, what have you done?"

Mike started walking down hill to see if the lake was in view, but couldn't see anything because of all the alders and cloud cover over the valley. The blurriness was going away and he could tell he was higher in altitude then at the cabin, and decided to walk parallel to his left. This was the direction he walked when he skirted the lake and this might lead him back to it, depending on what direction he came from to get to his current location.

A raven squawked from a nearby tree and flew off in the direction he had chosen.

"I hope you're leading me in the right direction, buddy," he said as the bird flew away.

After a few hours of walking he came to a place in the rocks that looked like a good place to stop for the night. He was hungry, thirsty and hurt worse than ever, but knew he should stop and hopefully find his way back the next morning. There were many rocks around the area, so he gathered some to build a small fire pit and looked for some wood.

After gathering as much wood as he could he heard something familiar, the faint sound of water moving through rocks. He left the pile of wood before he lit it and walked toward the sound. A hundred yards away was a stream moving down the mountain. This was exactly what he needed. He now had water to drink and a path that should take him back to the lake. He carefully knelt down and drank as much water as he could before he felt sick.

Mike walked back to his new camp, lit the fire and tried to get some sleep.

The next morning came quick. The fire was out, and he was cold and hungry. Once back at the lake he hoped he would recognize something. He was feeling a little better, but was having a hard time moving his arm. He didn't want to look at it. He knew it was bad.

As the stream came into view again, he carefully negotiated his way down beside it after drinking from it again.

The stream continued to get bigger, so he decided he would cross it before it got too big. If this was the stream just up the lake from the cabin, he had it made. How he had walked so far and not known how he got there, he still didn't know.

Mike could finally see the lake as he went down the mountain and through the low clouds, but didn't recognize anything.

*Maybe when I get down to it,* he thought.

Once he got to the lake, he didn't remember seeing any of what lay before him. He visually scoured the area, looking up, down and across the lake. None of it was familiar. Mike decided to chance it and keep going southeast.

The footing was getting easier and the rocks turned into tundra and then beach. He really needed his cane, but the sticks he had found along the way would have to work. The injury had healed to a point that he could walk with little help, but wanted to keep as much weight off it as possible.

He continued on, drinking right out of the streams he crossed, thinking that the water fresh from the mountains would be cleaner. He hadn't eaten in days and didn't feel as hungry anymore.

"Is this good or bad?" he wondered. "It can't be good, I need food."

The lake started taking small bends on the shore that he would have to skirt all the way around in order to keep going. This was taking its toll and he was getting very tired and walking less each day.

One morning after waking up on the ground by a tree that he thought he had climbed, he got up and started walking around yet another bend in the lake. Once getting to the other side, he decided he would rest.

Mike rounded the small bend, crossed over a log and couldn't believe what lay in front of him.

He fell to his knees and yelled, "NO!"

There was a larger bend in the lake and he would have to walk around it. He lay on the ground for a while and finally decided to go on. He was starving, exhausted and beaten but had to keep going.

"I'll find something to eat soon," he told himself.

Mike continued through the woods that skirted the lake. Parts of the shore were rocky or had logs piled up, so walking through the woods was the best route in his condition. It would take the rest of the day and all of the next to go all the way around the water. This was a major setback and he didn't know if he could make it. He went as far as he could before it started getting dark. Mike made himself a small den on the beach out of a deadfall, and tucked himself in for the night.

He still wondered how he had gotten so turned around that night on his way to get the ducks. Why was he not able to find the way back again? If he had been able to get back to the warmth and shelter, he would eventually be saved, he was sure of it. But it didn't matter now. He was here and had to make the best of what he had.

He woke up sometime later and heard the sound of a plane's engine, or so he thought. He looked around and heard nothing else after a minute, but a squirrel chattering and he couldn't see anything.

"You're imagining things again. Keep it together," he told himself.

It was almost dark, so he tried to go back to sleep.

# Chapter Eighteen: Reality

A chirping squirrel woke Mike the next morning, so he warily rose and attempted to stretch out his soreness.

"It was probably you that woke me last night, wasn't it?" he asked the squirrel before it bounded off on the tree branches.

He took a sip of water from the lake even though he knew he shouldn't, splashed some on his face and started walking along what looked like a game trail through the woods. His head was pounding, but he had taken care not to dehydrate so it was probably the lack of food and the ache of his body. His throat was dry and the sores in his mouth were bleeding. He hoped he would find something to eat soon. His leg was still feeling better, but his arm was like its own inferno of pain.

He was walking along with his head down. His neck was very stiff after using a branch as a pillow again. He heard something in front of him. As he looked up, he came face to face with a man wearing glasses and a fishing cap with flies in it.

Mike quickly pulled and raised his revolver and in a scratchy voice yelled, "Are you real?"

He was shaking badly and the revolver was moving side to side as he pointed it.

The man was carrying a fishing pole and a cup of coffee. His mouth was wide open as they looked at each other. He swallowed hard and started shaking while dropping his pole and putting his hands up, hanging onto his coffee cup, trying not to spill it.

"Are you real?" Mike pleaded again, cocking the hammer on the weapon.

Mike only had one bullet left in his revolver after his run-ins with the wild animals along the way. He had been considering using it on himself for the last few days. Mike had been seeing things he knew couldn't be there and didn't know if this guy was real or not.

"I...I am," said the man.

Mike started laughing and fell backward against a tree.

The man walked over to him and asked, "Are you okay?"

"My plane crashed," Mike explained. "I've been out here for a long time."

"I'll go and get help," said the man.

"Don't leave me," Mike responded franticly, reaching out for him.

"I'll be right back. I promise," said the man, holding his nose at the obvious smell emanating from Mike.

"Hey," said Mike.

"Yes?" said the man.

"I'm Mike," he offered, as he reached out his hand, wanting to know if the man was really there.

"Glad to meet you Mike. My name's Stan," he said.

The two men shook hands and Stan left to get help. He was back in about ten minutes with their guide and his friends.

All the men took to their knees around Mike and started giving him food and water. The guide got on his satellite phone and called the Alaska State Troopers.

Mike ate some food and drank some water from a water bottle they handed him, and that was the last thing he remembered, except for a few blurry visions along the way. The men carrying him to the beach and the helicopter that came to pick him up were some of them. He was in and out throughout the flight to Anchorage in the Coast Guard helicopter that was sent to get him.

The local news channel on the TV kept reporting on the missing California man that had braved the Alaska wilderness for forty-seven days after surviving a plane crash on his way to go spring brown bear hunting.

"The plane had crashed just two miles northwest of the camp site that they were headed to after they entered Lake Clark Pass on the west side of Cook Inlet. There were coolers of food, propane and almost everything this man would have needed to survive for weeks if he had made it there, investigators told us," said the reporter. "The crashed plane was found just three days after the mayday had been received. The search was called off after ten days. There had been no sign of Mike Sullivan at the crash site and after finding the mutilated body of Ted Sanderson, Alaska State Troopers and others in the search party decided that they might never find him. This is an amazing story of survival, Rita."

"Yes it is, Will," said the other reporter.

"Stay with us as we continue to cover this miraculous story, after these messages," the first reporter said.

There was a map behind the two news casters that showed the campsite, the crash site and the probable route Mike had taken to find help, based on where he had been found. He would learn that the emergency transponder had activated when they crashed and stayed active, but because of the weather the search party couldn't get to the mountain until the fog lifted. The transponder was in the tail section that had sheared off and was found at the bottom of the mountain with quite a bit of the gear Mike had looked for.

Some of the planes he heard while trekking through the tundra had been searching for him. If he had stayed where he had crashed, the search party might not have gotten to him before the cold or wolves had ended his journey. Leaving and going through all he did is what saved his life.

The second cabin and the S.O.S. fire had been located soon after he had wandered into the woods and couldn't find the cabin again. He was told that the infection and fever he had were more than likely the reason for him wandering off and getting lost.

"Can you turn that off, please?" asked Mike, as he woke up and squeezed Rachael's hand, reassuring himself all of this was real. She must have been holding it while he was out of it. When he spoke, he could feel his lips crack as they were still blistered from exposure.

She just started talking like she always did, and he knew at this point he wouldn't get a word in.

He hardly heard what she said. He was looking her over, taking in the recent upgrades to her wardrobe. *New dress, new jewelry and a perfect new tan*, he thought. "Figures," he said out loud.

She stopped talking and looked at him. "What figures?" she asked.

"It figures that you would look so good."

Rachael smiled at him and said, "You're a hero sweetheart and..."

"Why? Because I didn't die like Ted did? I survived," said Mike, cutting her off mid- sentence. "It doesn't mean I'm a hero. I'm lucky, and that's all."

Not knowing how to respond to this and trying to remember what the doctors had told her about being patient with him, Rachel left to go get the boys out in the waiting area. They had flown up from California as soon as they got the call that Mike had been found. Even more family from different places around the country were on the way, too. Mike had about thirty people that had been at the hospital day and night since he had been rescued. Some people were familiar and others were relatives of Ted's that he barely knew.

Mike had left on his hunting trip weighing 227 pounds and was down to 154 now. He was underweight and malnourished.

He had been asleep for almost two days since arriving. He came in extremely dehydrated and his arm was severely infected. He was lucky to be alive and be able to keep his arm too. If he hadn't been rescued when he had, he wouldn't have lasted more than a few more days, according to the doctors.

The boys came rushing in to the hospital room and were ecstatic to see their dad.

They both stopped in the doorway and stared. Mike looked over at them, wondering what they were doing.

"I don't think they've ever seen you with a beard," said Rachael, as she walked in behind them.

"Have you two been good for your mom and everyone else?" Mike asked them.

"We have," said James while Jack texted on his cell phone, but put it away quickly.

They could tell that there was something different about their dad, but were still excited to see him. The boys sat on either side of the bed and talked to Mike for over an hour, catching up on the lost time. After a while, Rachael told them to go back out to the waiting room and let everyone know that their dad was okay.

"I love you," said Rachael when the boys left the room.

"I've loved you since the first time I laid eyes on you," said Mike.

Rachael broke down crying and told him how sorry she was for the argument they had before he left on his trip.

"I looked at your picture on my cell phone many times before it died. All I could think about was getting home to you and the boys."

Rachael sat there crying and squeezing his hand. She finally got up and said she was going to the bathroom to clean up.

When she left the room, he hit the call button and a nurse came into the room soon after.

"What can I do for you Mr. Sullivan?"

"Can you get my doctor please? I want to ask him some questions."

"She," said the nurse. "I'll go see if I can find her."

"Thank you," he replied.

A few minutes later a petite blonde walked into the room.

"How can I help you, Mike?" she asked with a southern accent.

"How bad are my injuries and when can I get out of here?"

"Don't you like the food?" she asked with a smile. "Straight to the point, I like that. You're healing nicely. We're all impressed with how you were able to care for your injuries without adequate medical supplies. We had a harder time scraping away all the infected and dead skin on your arm, but it's doing much better and I would say just a few more days in here until the antibiotics get into your system effectively. Then you can go home. You're one lucky guy. Most people wouldn't have lasted so long out there. Our fine state can be very unforgiving. You get some rest now."

"Thank you for all that you've done."

"Just doin' my job, honey."

The doctor left and Mike turned the light off with the remote next to his right hand. He had a lot to think about, but was thankful to be back in civilization.

Rachael walked out of the bathroom just as the doctor was leaving. She walked over to Mike's bed and slid in beside him.

The next few days, with so many people in and out of his room, were agonizing. Many reporters wanted to talk to him, but he declined the interviews. Rachael kept people away from the room that tried to get in to talk with him. The boys spent a lot of time talking and laughing by his bedside.

Mike got up one morning and went into the bathroom. He had already seen himself in the mirror, but decided it was time to shave his beard. After calling a nurse into his room and asking for a razor and scissors, he went to work cutting the hair short and shaving it all off. He would get a haircut when he got back home.

When he was released from the hospital, Mike thanked all the nurses and his doctor as he was rolled by the nurses' station toward the front door. He saw dozens of people out front with cameras and asked if he could be taken out a different way. The nurse pushing him in the wheelchair asked a security guard to tell everyone up front that Mike had to go to the pharmacy and get a prescription and would be right back to answer questions, allowing an escape out a side door to the rental van that was waiting.

Mike knew he had to get on a plane to go back home. He wasn't even nervous, even though Rachael said it would be understandable if he were.

"If it's my time, then that's when I'll die," he told her. "I'm still here for a reason."

The grocery store chain that Mike worked for chartered a plane to take them all back to California. This was a charity write off for them, and advertisement. Mike knew this all too well and couldn't blame them. He was glad that he wasn't flying commercial where he would have to put up with people wanting to talk to him and ask him questions. He just wanted to be left alone and heal.

The flight back was uneventful and everyone aboard the plane was glad for it.

The boys slept most of the way back, and Rachael tried to spark a conversation with her husband a few times.

"I've got a question for you," she started just after they left Anchorage. "What was with the two decaying animal feet in your coat pocket that were found?"

Mike smiled at the question. "I forgot about those," he replied. "I cut them off of a rabbit I killed the day after the crash. I thought the boys might want to have lucky rabbit feet like I had growing up."

That was a nice thought, but I heard the nurse that pulled them out almost lost her lunch.

The two of them were laughing about it and continued to talk and catch up the rest of the flight.

As per Mike's request, there were only a few people from corporate waiting to great them when they landed. He didn't want a big show when he got back.

"I want to drive," Mike told Rachael as they approached their Ford SUV in long-term parking.

"Are you sure?" she asked while handing him the keys.

"I've been dreaming about this," he said as he took the keys and kissed her on the cheek.

The family got in the vehicle and drove back home.

# Chapter Nineteen: Home Sweet Home

Back to reality was a bit of a transition. Mike would wake Rachael while having nightmares about his ordeal. He would wake up screaming and sweating profusely.

"What about going to see a counselor?" she asked him one morning while eating breakfast, not long after Mike's return.

"You mean a shrink? I don't think that would help, I'm not crazy," he said.

"I wasn't implying that you were. What about a support group?"

"I'm willing to bet that there aren't many support groups for people who were lost in the wild for months," he responded sarcastically.

Rachael walked over to him and said, "I'm just trying to help," then made her way out of the room.

"I know you are," Mike said softly, as she left.

While letting his wounds heal, he had a lot of time on his hands. He didn't know if he wanted to go back to work at the store and told corporate he would be making a decision soon.

It was summertime in southern California and Mike was happy to be enjoying the hot weather. The air conditioner in the house was a nice treat, but wasn't the same as the meat locker at the store.

After finally agreeing to seek counseling, Mike felt more comfortable talking to Rachael and the boys about his experiences. The counselor was able to help him realize his potential and cope with what had happened. Many things were brought to light as they starting talking to each other again.

It turned out she hadn't been cheating on him before he had left. She had been attending a pottery class at night with some girlfriends and the showers she took before going to bed was to wash off the clay dust and smell from the kiln. Mike was relieved and embarrassed when he found out.

Rachael had started working as a receptionist at an accounting firm not long after Mike's crash in order to be able to pay the bills and take care of the boys in his absence. She continued to do this while he recovered and figured out what his next step would be.

In the weeks that followed his rescue and return to civilization, Mike was already making plans to put his boys in a survival school or have them join the Boy Scouts or something along those lines. After his experience, he decided to get certified to be able to teach others how to survive in the Alaska wilderness before they went there.

Working at the grocery store was soon a thing of the past. He wanted to start his own website and work with hiking and hunting guides, as well as organizations all over the state and possibly the country. He designed a survival pack with everything you would need to survive for months in the wild. After his experience, he was approached by TV show hosts to appear for interviews and talk about the ordeal. He declined all of them, even when he was offered money.

In order to get his story out there and to help others, he did agree to a book deal and was told it might be turned into a movie one day. He just laughed and said, "Who would want to make a movie about me?"

Mike was considering hiring someone for technical support on a friend's recommendation. She ran a small business out of her home building websites and was supposed to be very good.

Mike called the number and a soft voice answered.

"Web Solutions, this is Shellie," said the voice.

"Uh...Yes, I was given your number by a friend. He said you could build a website for me."

"Yes I can. Would you like to set up an appointment for a consultation?"

"I would," said Mike, "Thank you."

"What works for you?"

"I don't have much going on, I can show up anytime, really."

"You are for real, right?" Shellie asked.

"Yes, I really am. I can pay up front if you need me to."

"Not necessary, who am I speaking with?"

"My name's Mike."

"Okay Mike and a contact number?"

The appointment was set up for the following morning at ten a.m.

"Why the hell were you so nervous? You sounded like an idiot," Mike said to himself after hanging up. "You've been gone too long."

Mike realized he was still talking to himself and was afraid people would think he was crazy and he might end up in a psycho ward somewhere.

The counseling was helping, but talking to people and being around them was still difficult for him.

The next morning, Mike showed up for the meeting early, as usual. Shellie answered the door wearing a long blue skirt. She greeted him and invited him in. Her long brown hair was waving as she walked away from him.

"I hope this is okay, coming to my home and all," she said.

"It is. Why would you ask that?"

"I've had some people not like the fact that I work out of here and question whether I can get the job done right and on time," said Shellie.

"I don't have a problem with it. I actually like the fact that you're saving money by not having an office, and more than likely feel more comfortable here anyway."

"I do, actually. Would you like some coffee, tea or anything else to drink?"

"I'm fine, thank you," said Mike.

"So, Mike, what kind of business are you in and do you have any ideas for your site?"

"I have an idea and that's as far as I've gotten. Can you help me?"

"I'm sure I can, tell me about your idea."

Mike told Shellie a little about his ordeal and she remembered reading about it. She liked the idea of selling a product that was already out there, but marketing it the way Mike wanted to. By adding certain items to a pack that he knew from experience were needed in extreme survival situations, it should work well.

Shellie was very good at what she did. Not only at the web design, but working with the customer's ideas and figuring out the best way to sell them.

Mike had designed a survival tool made out of titanium that, when unfolded, turned into an axe, saw, shovel and even a fishing pole. The handle held many basic supplies, like matches, hooks, line, weights and much more. The tool could be taken apart to make the different tools and reassembled to make a small, compact piece that went in one of his many sized packs with many other survival tools.

The company that Mike started after selling his story was called Survival Inc. Rachael stood by her husband's decision to start the business and take care of all of them. She could see that he had returned a stronger man, and told him so.

His physical wounds were healing, but his mind would take longer. Getting his life back on track was the goal, and Mike was slowly accomplishing it with his family by his side.

Special thanks to:

Eric Cox - For your continued support with your thoughts.

Joseph Robertia – For taking on this project and helping to make it the best it could be.

Jenny Neyman - For your detailed editing of my stories.

Melanie Noblin – For the fantastic work on the covers.

Createspace Team Two – For putting up with all of my questions and helping me through the process each time

This is the fifth book of many that will be written. I wouldn't be able to do any of this without the support of all of you.

Thank You!

# About The Author

Travis Wright was born and raised in a small, Oregon town, where his love of the outdoors began. He grew up hunting and fishing in the rural Northwest, a lifestyle that transferred easily to a life in the Last Frontier. Wright has been in Alaska for 22 years, and now lives in Soldotna with his wife and five children, a daughter and four teenage boys.

When he's not busy with his family or trekking through the backcountry, Wright works in the retail gun store he's owned and operated for 14 years. He is an NRA-certified instructor and enjoys teaching others gun skill and safety.

Wright's interest in firearm technology as well as his active duty in the Marine Corps infantry are both influential in his work as a writer. While Wright has written poetry off and on for most of his adult life, his work as a novelist began in 2010 with the survival story, "Uncertain Times." Since putting that work to rest, he hasn't stopped writing. Wright's lifelong active imagination and curiosity have found their outlet in storytelling.

More ideas for stories are emerging all the time. Look for them to be published soon.

26809595R00088

Made in the USA
San Bernardino, CA
04 December 2015